HALF-PAST SEVEN STORIES

ROBERT GORDON ANDERSON

Half-Past Seven Stories

Robert Gordon Anderson

© 1st World Library – Literary Society, 2004
PO Box 2211
Fairfield, IA 52556
www.1stworldlibrary.org
First Edition

LCCN: 2004195348

Softcover ISBN: 1-4218-0182-5
Hardcover ISBN: 1-4218-0082-9
eBook ISBN: 1-4218-0282-1

Purchase *"Half-Past Seven Stories"*
as a traditional bound book at:
www.1stWorldLibrary.org/purchase.asp?ISBN=1-4218-0182-5

1st World Library Literary Society is a nonprofit organization dedicated to promoting literacy by:

- Creating a free internet library accessible from any computer worldwide.
- Hosting writing competitions and offering book publishing scholarships.

Readers interested in supporting literacy through sponsorship, donations or membership please contact:
literacy@1stworldlibrary.org
Check us out at: www.1stworldlibrary.ORG
and start downloading free ebooks today.

Half-Past Seven Stories
contributed by Tim, Ed & Rodney
in support of
1st World Library Literary Society

TO

SARAH DAVIS ANDERSON

Not that this dedication is in itself so great an honor, but because the youngsters' choice, "Aunt Sally!" is indeed a tribute to the loving heart which has made so many little ones happy.

CONTENTS

INTRODUCTION - "THE TOP OF THE MORNING"

"The top o' the morning!"

That's what the Toyman used to say. And I am sure if you ever go to the White House with the Green Blinds by the Side of the Road the Toyman will say it still, whatever the weather.

And when you hear him call that over the fence so cheerily, from his smile you will know at once what he means, - that he wishes for you the *very* top of the morning, not only the finest of weather, but the best of happiness and fun, in whatever you do and wherever you go.

If you have read all about him in the *Seven O'Clock Stories* you will remember his name. Of course, it won't matter whether you've read them or not - you can make his acquaintance at any time - but the sooner the better, for, as all who know him will tell you, he's worth knowing.

His name is Frank Clarke, but his real name isn't really as real as the one the children gave him, - "the Toyman." For he is forever making them things, - kites and tops, and sleds and boats, and jokes and happiness and laughter.

His face is as brown as saddle leather, with a touch of apple red in it from the sun. There are creases in it, too, because he laughs and jokes so much. Sometimes when he appears to be solemn you want to laugh most, for he's only pretending to be solemn. And, best of all, if you hurt yourself, or if your pet doggie hurts himself, the Toyman will know how to fix it, to "make it all well" again.

The Three Happy Children love him. That's what we always call them, though they, too, have other names - funny ones, you will think, - Jehosophat, Marmaduke, and Hepzebiah Green, but they are family names and came from some very old uncles and aunts.

They still live in the White House with the Green Blinds by the Side of the Road - that is, when they aren't sliding down hill, or fishing in the Pond, or riding on the hay, or to town with the Toyman and Ole Methusaleh. Mother and Father are still there. Home wouldn't be home without them. And they have many playmates and friends - of all sorts - two-legged and four-legged, in serge and corduroy, in feathers and fur.

What they all did, the fun they had, and the trouble they got in and out of, you'll find if you turn these pages.

One thing more - a secret - in *absolute* confidence, though. - After all, it isn't really so *very* necessary to read these stories at *Half-Past Seven*. You can read them, or be read to, "any ole time," as the Toyman used to say - Monday morning, Thursday noon, or Saturday night - as long as it doesn't interfere with those lessons.

Robert Gordon Anderson

Still, the very best time is at twilight in summer when the lights and the fireflies begin to twinkle through the dusk, or in the winter around the fire just before you go to bed - with Father or Mother - or the Toyman.

*   *   *   *   *

P.S. -

The Toyman says to send his love and "The Top o' the Morning."

I

THE LITTLE LOST FOX

Marmaduke was sitting on the fence. He wasn't thinking of anything in particular, just looking around. Jehosophat called to him from the barnyard, -

"Come'n an' play 'I spy.'"

But Marmaduke only grumbled, -

"Don't want to."

"Well, let's play 'Cross Tag' then," Jehosophat suggested.

"Don't want to," repeated his brother again, not very politely.

Jehosophat thought for a moment, then he suggested something worth-while:

"I'll tell you what, let's play 'Duck-on-the-Rock.'"

Now as every boy in the world - at least in America - knows, that is a wonderful game, but Marmaduke only said very crossly, -

"I don't want to play any of your ol' games." Now when Marmaduke acted that way there must have been something the matter. Perhaps he had gobbled down his oatmeal too fast - in great big gulps - when he should have let the Thirty White Horses "champ, champ, champ," all those oats. They were cooked oats, but then the Thirty White Horses, unlike Teddy and Hal and ole Methusaleh, prefer cooked oats to raw.

Perhaps he had eaten a green apple. Sometimes he did that, and the tart juice puckered his mouth all up, and - what was worse - puckered his stomach all up, too.

Any way, he felt tired and out-of-sorts; tired of his toys, tired of all the games, even such nice ones as "Duck-on-the-rock" and "Red Rover."

There was nothing to do but sit on the fence.

Still, the world looked pretty nice from up there. It always looked more interesting from a high place, and sometimes it gave you an excited feeling. Of course, the big elm was a better perch, or the roof of the barn, and Marmaduke often wondered what it would be like to see the world from a big balloon, but the fence was good enough. It curved up over a little hill, and he could see lots of the world from there.

He looked over towards the West, where the Sun marched into his barn every night. Fatty Hamm declared that the Sun kept a garage behind that hill, but Marmaduke insisted it was a *barn*, for he liked horses best, and the Sun *must* drive horses. There was a real hill there, not little like the one where he sat on the fence, but a big one, 'most as big as a mountain, Marmaduke thought. Sometimes it was green, and sometimes grey or blue, and once or twice he had seen it almost as purple as a pansy.

But it was Fall now, and the hill had turned brown. Over it he could see little figures moving. He looked at them very carefully, with one eye shut to see them the better. Then he decided that the bigger ones were men on horses, the little ones dogs. They all looked tiny because they were so far away.

As they came nearer and the sun shone on them, he was pretty sure the men had red coats. Could they be *soldiers*?

Just then the Toyman came by, with coils of wire and clippers in his hand. He was on his way to mend the fence in the North Pasture.

"'Llo Toyman!" said Marmaduke.

"Howdy, little fellow!" replied the Toyman, "what are you doing there? Settin' on the top of the world and enjoyin' yourself?"

"I was wondering what those men over there were doing." And the boy waved his hand towards the little black figures on the hill.

"Why, that's the hunt," explained the Toyman. "The rich folks, having nothing better to do, are killin' time."

Marmaduke was puzzled.

"Are they really hunting *Time*?" he asked. "I thought maybe they were hunting lions or tigers."

Robert Gordon Anderson

"No, not today," the Toyman responded, "I'm sorry to disappoint you, but they're only after Reddy."

"Reddy Toms?" the little boy exclaimed. "*Why, whatever did he do?*"

Now Reddy Toms was a boy in his own class, and you could always tell him a long way off because his head was covered with red hair as thick as a thatched roof, and his face was spotted all over, like a snake's, with freckles.

However, the Toyman said it was all a mistake.

"No, not that tad," he explained, "it's Reddy *Fox* they're after."

"What!" exclaimed Marmaduke. "Does it take all those big men to hunt one little fox?"

"It seems so, son," the Toyman returned, "but that's the way of the world."

"Well, I think it's mean," insisted Marmaduke. "Those men are nothing' but - but - *dumbbells*!"

The Toyman threw back his head and laughed. That was a new expression to him, but it was a perfectly good one. You see, the big boys in school used it when they thought anyone was particularly stupid or mean. But the Toyman must have understood it anyway, for he went on, -

"That's my sentiments exactly. I don't suppose they mean to be cruel, but they don't give little Reddy half a chance - and he's so small! Now if it was lions or tigers, as you suggest, why, that would be different."

"You bet it would!" Marmaduke replied. "I just wish it *was*." Now, of course, he should have said "were," as the teacher in the Red Schoolhouse was forever telling him, but a little boy can't always remember correct English when a hunt is coming so close.

"Just set tight, boy, and you'll see their red coats soon."

And, waving his clippers, the Toyman went on his way to the North Pasture.

But Marmaduke didn't need any advice. He had spotted those red coats already. They were much nearer now, for they rode very fast. Already the horses were leaping the fence of the Miller Farm, and the dogs were crisscrossing over the field, making lots of letter W's as they ran - hundreds of them, Marmaduke was sure. And they followed something - something so small he could hardly see what it was. But he guessed it must be Reddy.

So many fences they leaped, and so many stone walls! Now they were near the Brook, and yes, he could see the red coats, very bright and plain now.

And then he spied Reddy. His coat wasn't as gay as those the men wore. Theirs were bright like cherries, and his was the color of chestnuts. It seemed such a shame to want his poor little coat when the men had such nice ones themselves.

"Cracky!" he exclaimed. One of the "ole hunters" had fallen in the Brook. And Marmaduke hoped that red coat would get soaked and soaked and run like the stockings Mother had bought from the pedlar. And he hoped that "ole hunter" would get wet to the skin, and shiver and shiver, and have to call in the doctor who'd prescribe the very worst medicine there was in the world. It would serve that "ole hunter" right if he'd almost die. But Marmaduke hoped the poor horse wouldn't break his leg. It wasn't the horses' fault they were chasing Reddy.

Now the hunters were lost in Jake Miller's Woods. All he could see were patches of red, here and there, in the bushes, but he heard the deep voices of the dogs, all the time, calling and calling.

Then all-of-a-sudden something happened. And Marmaduke liked all-of-a-sudden things to happen - they were so exciting.

A little streak of fur, with tail flying behind like a long pretty hat brush, galloped across the Apgar field, then the very field where Marmaduke sat, perched on the fence.

The dogs were right after Reddy, running hard, too, but they were two fields farther back. Reddy, you see, had fooled them in that wood, and he had gotten a good headstart.

My, how Reddy was running!

Marmaduke stood up on the fence and shouted:

"Hooray, go it Reddy!"

He shouted so hard, and waved his hands so excitedly that he tumbled off his perch, and lay still for a second.

He was frightened, too, but he forgot all about the bump on his forehead, and picked himself up, and ran after Reddy across the field towards the barnyard, which, fortunately, was just on the other side.

"Oooooooohhhhh!" - a very deep "Ooooooohhhh!" came from behind him from the throats of the dogs. They were only one field away now, and it sounded as if they were pretty mad.

But Reddy had reached the corner of the field where the blackberry bushes lined the fence. Now usually Reddy would have looked all around those bushes until he found an opening; then he would have stepped daintily through it. But he didn't do that today, oh no! You see his family has a great reputation for wisdom, and Reddy must have been just as wise as the man in Mother Goose, for he neither stopped nor stayed, but jumped right in those brambles and managed somehow to get through the rails of the fence to the other side. He left part of his pretty red coat in the briars. However, that was better than leaving it *all* to those dogs who were howling not far behind.

And now the Little Fox found himself near the barn and flew towards it so fast that his legs fairly twinkled as he ran.

The Foolish White Geese were taking their morning waddle, and Reddy ran plump into them. Now there was nothing that he liked better to eat than nice fat goose. Still, he didn't wait, but left them beating their wings and stretching their long necks to hiss, hiss, hiss, as they scattered in all directions. I guess Reddy wished his legs were as long as their necks.

Robert Gordon Anderson

Now in the old days when rich folks lived in castles and robber knights quarreled and fought every day of the week, there were always places of sanctuary, where any man could be safe from harm. That is just what Reddy saw in front of him, a place of sanctuary for himself.

It was funny, but it had been prepared by little Wienerwurst. And Wienerwurst was really Reddy's enemy, for all dogs like to chase foxes whenever they get the chance. It was a little hole, just the right size for Wienerwurst, just the right size for Reddy. The little yellow doggie wasn't there now. He had dug it that morning to catch the big rat hiding somewhere below the floor of the barn. He had started to build a tunnel under the wall, and had been a long time working at it when Mother Green came from the house. She carried a fine large bone, with lots of meat left on it, too. And, of course, when the little dog smelled that bone and meat, much as he liked rats, he just had to leave his work at the tunnel and run straight for the bone, leaving the hole waiting for Reddy.

Straight into it Reddy ran, just as Marmaduke and the big dogs reached the fence and the blackberry bushes, all at the same time. Now Marmaduke could have cried because the hunter dogs would reach the hole before he could get there and cover it up, and they would reach down into that hole and drag Reddy out by his pretty red coat and eat him all up.

But when he stuck his head through the rail he saw help coming. Jehosophat was there and he had heard those bad dogs and seen them, too, coming on with their big mouths open and their tongues hanging out as if they wanted to swallow Reddy down in one gulp.

And Jehosophat could see the redcoats on the horses not far away. They had reached the big oak in the field and were coming on very fast.

He looked around. There was the very thing. A nice, broad cover of an egg-crate. It would fit exactly. So, quick as a wink, Jehosophat picked it up and clapped it over the hole. Then he looked around again. It wasn't quite safe yet. But there was the big rock which they used for "Duck-on-the-rock." The very thing! It was almost more than he could manage, that rock, but he pulled and he tugged, and he tugged and he pulled, 'til he had it safe on the crate-cover over the hole - and Reddy was saved!

It was just in time, too, for the dogs had come barking and yelping and bellowing, and now all they could do was to sniff, sniff, sniff around that hole.

Then over the fence into the barnyard jumped the horses; and Marmaduke came running up; and the Toyman rushed over from the field; and Father came out of the barn; and Mother flew out of the house; and Rover and Brownie and Wienerwurst raced from the pond, each one to see what all the hullabaloo was about.

What they did see was the two boys standing guard in front of the hole to protect little Reddy, and the big hunter dogs jumping up on them with their paws and growling most terribly. It was a wonder that the boys weren't frightened enough to run away, but they didn't. They just stood their ground. Still, they were glad enough to see Father and the Toyman close by.

And now one of the men in redcoats had dismounted

from his horse, and Marmaduke called to him, -

"You shan't touch Reddy, you *shan't*!"

He was half crying, too, not for himself, but for Reddy.

The man was taking off his cap. He was very polite, and he bowed to Mother.

"We'll pay for all damages, Madam, but let us have the brush."

The boys thought that was funny, calling their mother "madam," when everybody in the neighborhood called her "Mis' Green." And what did he want a brush for? To brush his fine cap and red coat or his shiny boots? Or to wipe up Reddy out of his hole? However, the Toyman was whispering:

"He means Reddy's tail. That's what hunters call the brush."

When Marmaduke heard that, he grabbed tight hold of the Toyman's hand on one side and of his father's on the other, and shouted:

"Don't let them get Reddy!"

But Father was talking to the man. He called him "Mr. Seymour-Frelinghuysen," and both the boys wondered if all people with fine horses and shiny boots and red coats had to have long, funny-sounding names like that.

"It's all right about the damages, Mr. Seymour-Frelinghuysen," Father was saying, "but I guess we won't give up the fox today."

And Father smiled down at Marmaduke, and oh, wasn't that little boy relieved and happy, and his brother, too! As for the Toyman, he had a funny twinkle in his eyes.

Of course, there was a lot of grumbling on the part of the redcoats, and a lot of barking and growling from the big hunter dogs, but the men had to get on their horses and call off their dogs and ride away.

"I guess they knew they were in the wrong," said Jehosophat, after they had tied up Rover and Brownie and Wienerwurst, and taken the stone and board away from Reddy's hole.

Then they looked in the hole-but no Reddy!

Meanwhile the Toyman had gone into the barn.

"Come here!" he shouted.

So they ran in, and there, in the corner, hidden under the hay was Reddy, all muddy from the brook and torn from the briars. His eyes looked very bright, but they looked pitiful too.

The Toyman put out his hand and stroked his fur. At first Reddy showed his teeth and snapped at the Toyman just like a baby wolf. But that hand came towards him so quietly, and the voice sounded so gentle, that Reddy lay still. You see, the Toyman somehow understood how to treat foxes and all kinds of animals just as well as he did boys, little or big.

"What *doesn't* that man know?" Mother had said

Robert Gordon Anderson

once, and right she was, too.

It took some time to train Reddy, for, although he was very small, he was very wild. However, the Toyman managed to tame him. Perhaps it was because the Little Lost Fox was wounded and sore and hurt all over. Anyway, he seemed to appreciate what the Toyman did for him, for all he was a little wild child of the fields and the forests.

They built him a house, all for himself, and a fence of wire. It was great fun to see him poking his sharp nose through the holes and stepping around so daintily on his pretty little feet.

He always had such a wise look. In fact, he was too wise altogether, for one day he was gone, through some little hole he had dug under his fence. - And they never saw him again - at least, they haven't to this day.

At first the three children felt very sad about this, but when the Toyman explained it, they saw how everything was all right.

"You see," the Toyman said, "he's happier in the woods and fields than being cooped up here."

Marmaduke thought about that for a moment.

"Anyway," he began, "anyway, -"

"Yes?" said Mother, trying to help him out.

"Anyway, I'm glad we saved him from the ole redcoats," he finished.

And maybe Reddy will visit them again some day. Stranger things than that have happened. So, who knows!

Robert Gordon Anderson

II

THE BIG BOBSLED

Teddy the Buckskin Horse and Hal the Red Roan had just come in the yard. They were drawing a big load of lumber from the mill which stood in the woods on the north branch of the River.

Just before he unloaded the boards and planks back by the barn, the Toyman picked out a few of the finest and carried them into his shop. That did look mysterious and suspicious - very pleasantly suspicious.

"I'll bet that's for us," declared Marmaduke.

"You just bet it is!" said his brother.

So each day for almost a week, they lingered around the shop, after school was out. But the Toyman never appeared until long after five. He had his cornhusking to do, and he wanted to get all the fall jobs finished before cold weather.

One week went by, then another. It was very provoking, thought the boys, to have to wait so long for that secret.

Jehosophat did try once to find out about it. He stopped

the Toyman as he was coming from the barn with a pail full of bubbly milk.

"Say, Toyman, what are those boards for?"

"What boards?" asked the Toyman - just as if he didn't know.

"Those boards you put in your workshop," both the boys answered together. It sounded like some chorus they had learned for Commencement.

"Ho ho!" laughed the Toyman, "ask me no questions and I'll tell you no lies."

He was hopeless. He was forever making queer answers and queerer rhymes which Miss Prue Parsons the school teacher didn't at all approve. But Father said it didn't hurt the children as far as he could see - it just entertained them.

So the Toyman was answering:

"Ask me no questions an' I'll tell you no lies;
Gooseberries are sour but make very sweet pies."

The boys had to be content with that information, but it was very hard waiting.

There came a day when it rained, and the Toyman couldn't work in the fields, or paint the house, or mend the leaks in the roof of the barn. Of course, he might have fixed Old Methusaleh's harness, which badly needed repairs, but he looked at the sky and said, -

"It looks like snow. I ought to get at that - "

Then he bit his lip and the secret was still safe.

Very mysteriously he unlocked the door of his workshop. And the boys peeked in.

"Where's your ticket, Sonny?" he asked, seeing their two heads in the doorway. That was his way, you see, making a game out of everything.

"We haven't any, but oh, Toyman, let us in, *plee-a-sse.*"

"All right, but don't talk more than forty words to the minute, or I can't plane this straight," he said, working away at the boards.

They couldn't yet guess what *IT* was. And it took a good many hours from his work and chores for the Toyman to finish IT, whatever IT was. But after about a week they saw standing against the wall four boards about two feet long, curved like this:

And four more cross-pieces of a very ordinary shape:

And one cross-piece with handles:

Then one very long one like this:

The thing to do was to guess what they would make when put together.

Just then the Toyman arrived with three barrel hoops. And he worked away with his tools until the hoops were almost straight. Then he made little holes in them and nailed them with little nails, very neatly, on the four long curved pieces of wood. Then he fastened these curved pieces together by nailing the cross-pieces between. He fastened the other pair in the same way, and the affair began to look something like catamarans, those funny boats the geographies say folks use in Australasia.

But when he nailed the big board on and attached the steering gear, it was easy to see what all the time the Toyman had been planning to make. And when he painted the runners yellow with a little blue edge running around them, and the seat bright red, with a white star on it, they decided it was the finest bobsled in the world.

And, oh yes, he had to paint the word "Scud" in blue letters, right near the star.

Yes sir, there was no doubt about it, it was the finest bobsled in the world - the *whole* world, we mean.

And again the boys shouted, "Hooray!," together as in a chorus, not forgetting to add, - "And thank you, Toyman, *heaps*!"

Then they happened to think the bobsled was ready, but something else was missing - something very necessary, too.

"Now for the snow!" Jehosophat said.

"I can knock together a bobsled, sonny," the Toyman replied, "But I haven't any tools to make *that*."

So every night, when he said his prayers, Marmaduke added another sentence to "God bless Mamma an' Papa an' the Toyman an' Wienie an'" all the rest of his friends. Perhaps you can guess what it was. No? Well it sounded something like this:

"An' please, God, send us some snow, - a *whole lot of it*!"

Well, it came in about a week. On the twenty-third of November, to be exact.

It took only an hour to make the fields white, and only about three for the snow to pile deep enough to carry the new bobsled.

The Toyman looked at the sky, then at the ground, and then at his shop.

"Guess I'll knock off," he said. He was always knocking off work or something for the children.

But he had to stop their quarreling now. Each one wanted the honor of pulling the big bobsled first. For it was a thing to be proud of, with its yellow runners and the blue edge around them, and the red seat with the white star in the middle.

"You're as bad as the pigs in the corner pen," said the Toyman, "where are your manners?"

That settled it, of course. Turns! That was the proper way, and off they went.

But after all, "taking turns" wasn't as fine as the next thing the Toyman suggested.

"All jump on," he called, "and I'll be the cayuse."

That was a funny word he had learned out West, but by this time the children knew he meant *horse*. So the three, Jehosophat, Marmaduke, and Hepzebiah, sat on the red seat and were pulled through the snow, oh, ever so swiftly!

It was like riding through fairyland, for the branches above them were furred with white feathery snow, and the woods looked like some great lace design made by the Winter Queen who, they say, knits when the nights are cold and the Winter King is out at the club.

Soon they reached the hill. It was pretty steep and Jehosophat and Marmaduke wanted to get off and walk up so as to make it easier for the Toyman. He wouldn't hear of that, but just set his shoulders like Teddy in the shafts and puffed and pulled up hill.

On the fields the snow was light and feathery like powdered sugar, but on the hill it had been packed down hard by the coasters. There were so many of them, boys and girls from the neighborhood all around! Some were at the top, and some at the bottom, and some in the middle, sliding merrily down.

When the Three Happy Children reached the top of the hill the Toyman cried:

"I'll sit in front to steer and hold little Hepzebiah. You boys sit in back, Jehosophat at the end, and hold on to the grips."

Yes there were grips, too, for the Toyman hadn't forgotten anything that goes with a perfect sled.

Robert Gordon Anderson

"All aboard! Toot, toot!" he shouted, and Jehosophat yelled, -

"Clear the way!"

And down the hill they shot. It wasn't like any other kind of travel in the world. Perhaps it was more like flying than anything else, but that was funny, too, when you come to think of it, for when you fly you usually go up, and they were going down.

They reached the bottom all too soon, but the trip was worth the trouble of trudging back, especially as all the hard work was done by the Toyman.

When they reached the top again, once more he shouted, "All aboard, toot, toot!"

Some folks thought he was silly, and Mrs. Hamm, riding by in a buggy, on the road below, said to Mr. Hamm, -

"There's that good-for-nothing Frank Clark again, hollerin' like a wild Injun with all those children."

"Yes, Maria," agreed her husband. "I'd send him to the work'us if I was on the Township Committee."

But the Hamms, like many other people, were very stupid. Was the Toyman worth while? You just ask Jehosophat and Marmaduke and Hepzebiah and Wienerwurst, and hear what *they* have to say.

Once during that long and glorious afternoon they had trouble. Fatty Hamm started it. It was the only thing he was good at - trouble and eating. And, of course,

Reddy Toms and Dicky Means had to help him. Anyway, Fatty pushed Hepzebiah into a deep snowdrift - when he thought the Toyman wasn't looking. And Hepzebiah fell into the snowdrift head first so that only her legs could be seen, and they were kicking wildly in the air. Now the Toyman was busy untangling the rope, which had gotten mixed with the steering-gear, and he hadn't noticed Fatty and Reddy at their old tricks. But her two brothers pulled her out of the drift by her little kicking legs, and brushed her off and dried her tears. Then they went for Reddy and Fatty. Reddy ran away, but Fatty stood his ground, for he was much bigger than they. They had their fists clenched, and were going to punch him, very hard, I guess, when the Toyman looked up from his work and called, -

"What's the trouble, son?"

The boys explained it, but they kept their fists clenched just the same. They were rather excited, you see, and as soon as they were through telling the Toyman all about it, they wanted to pitch into "that ole Fatty."

But Fatty tried to lie out of it.

"She just fell herself," he said, half scared.

"She didn't, either," Jehosophat yelled, "he pushed her in." And he started to rush for the fat boy when the Toyman called, -

"Hold on there, let *me* settle it."

He came over, and squinted his eyes thoughtfully like a judge, while Fatty twisted and squirmed and

Robert Gordon Anderson

squirmed and twisted.

"I wouldn't hit him," said the Toyman, "Fatty's so fat it wouldn't do any good anyway. Your fists would only sink into him like dough. So I guess you'd better wash his face in the snow - *hard* now."

So they did - very *hard*, as the Toyman had told them.

"Why, he's actually blubbering, the great big booby," said Jehosophat, "shame!"

Now there's no word in the language in which boys and girls join more readily than this same word "Shame." So they all took up the chorus, everybody on that hill. You know that chorus, and your parents know it, and your grandparents, and great grandparents, too, sang it, long, long before you were born.

"Shame, shame, puddin' an' tame.
Everybody knows your name."

What pudding has to do with it probably none in the whole world knows. But it is a very effective song, and they one and all shouted it, dancing around Fatty and Reddy, and laughing at them; and the fat boy started to run away, yelling at the top of his lungs. But he stumbled over the bobsled, and the tangled ropes caught his feet and started him rolling down the hill. He didn't exactly roll, either, for he was so fat that he seemed to bounce like a rubber ball; and little Wienerwurst, who thought it all very fine sport, ran after him, nosing and snapping at him all the way down that hill. Then, when he reached the bottom, coward Fatty picked himself up and "made tracks" for home.

It was to - be sure, an odd sort of punishment that the Toyman ordered for Fatty. It was just such things that made Mr. and Mrs. Hamm and all the neighbors shake their heads over the Toyman and say he was crazy. But Jehosophat, who had heard it said that Solomon was a wonderful judge, knew one that could beat Solomon - and he was the Toyman.

Perhaps he was right. At all events, the children were ever so happy, as they coasted down, down the hill on that big bobsled, which they did till the stars came out, and, far over the fields, the supper bell sounded.

Robert Gordon Anderson

III

THE JOLLY ROGER

Marmaduke thought he knew now what it meant to be in jail. For three whole days he had had to stay in the house. For three whole days and nights, too, it had rained - "rained pitchforks." That is what Father said, but Marmaduke could see nothing but prongs. There were thousands of them, coming down through the air. *Where* were the handles? He looked a long time, thinking that perhaps they had gotten loose from the prongs and would come down afterwards, but never a handle came.

They must be having haying time, the folks in the sky, to use so many forks, he decided, and the sun must be shining for them, way up above the clouds, or they wouldn't have haying weather. But maybe, after all, it was wet there, too, and they had just grown disgusted, and were throwing their forks away, every last one of them.

Yes, it was pretty lonesome and dull, staying in the house like this. To be sure, once in a while, when the rain slackened a little and the pitchforks didn't come down so fast, he could put on his rubber boots and go out to the barn. But for most of the time he had been a prisoner - in jail.

He looked out at the Pond. So much water had fallen in it that it was swelling up like a pouter pigeon, or like the bowl that held the Chinese Lily, when he dropped pebbles in it.

My, how Duckie the Stepchild must like this weather! There he was now, and his father and his mother and all his relatives. All just letting the water run off their backs and having a grand time. But Father Wyandotte and all his family were sticking pretty close to the coops. Funny how ducks liked water and chickens didn't, all but the Gold Rooster on the top of the barn. *He* never seemed to mind it a bit. Marmaduke looked for him up in the sky, but he was almost hidden by the rain and the gray mist, and stood there on his high perch, swinging from East to North, and back again.

But he grew tired of watching the Gold Rooster, and looked up the pasture for his friend, the Brook. It wasn't hard to find, for it had grown so big and stretched almost to the fence-rails now, and was racing along towards the Pond, growing wider and wider every minute - just like Marmaduke's eyes.

"Crackey! Sposin' there should be a flood!" exclaimed Jehosophat.

"Wouldn't that be fine!" said Marmaduke.

"Fine!" Jehosophat cried. "What would you do? It might rise an' rise till the barnyard'd be covered, an' the road an' all the country an' the whole world."

"Like Noah's flood, you mean?"

"Yes, just like Noah's, only he isn't here to build any

ole ark for you to get on."

"I don't care," said Marmaduke stoutly.

"You don't care!" cried his brother. "Why, you'd drown, that's what you'd do!"

"No, I wouldn't either - " Marmaduke seemed very sure about this - "'cause," he started to explain.

"'Cause what?"

"'Cause the Toyman is as good as ole Noah any day," replied the little boy. "He could build an ark as big as a house, as big as the Church, an' the ducks'd get on an' the cows an' the horses an' -"

"Yes," interrupted his brother, "but don't you remember - there were only two of each kind. Now Hal an' Teddy could get on, but White Boots an' Ole Methusaleh'd have to stay off, an' Rover an' Brownie could go, but Wienerwurst couldn't - see?"

Marmaduke looked frightened at this - at the very thought of Wienerwurst, his little doggie, trying to swim around in a terrible flood.

"I'd hide him under my coat," he declared.

"You couldn't get on yourself," Jehosophat insisted, "I tell you an ark only takes two of each sort of people an' animals an' chickens and things. Now Mother and Father could go - that's two grown-ups, an' Hepzebiah an' me, but you an' Wienie would have to swim around in the water just as long as you could, then go under - way under, too," he added.

Perhaps he was only teasing, but Marmaduke didn't take it quite that way. It seemed very serious. Then suddenly he had a bright idea.

"You forgot the *Toyman*," he shouted, "and that makes another two, for the Toyman an' I are just alike. Didn't Mother say, - 'He's nothing but a boy.' So I'd sneak Wienie under my coat - if it was ol' Noah's ark - an' if it was the Toyman's, why he'd let me in anyway."

Jehosophat had no answer at all for this, and all they could do now was to watch the rain and the Pond and the Brook, but Marmaduke was very happy picturing to himself the big Ark which the Toyman would build, and how he would help, and the fine time, too, he and all the animals would have, living together under the very same roof.

Of course, the rain had to stop some time. It always does in the end. And on the sixth day the Sun came out jolly and warm again, and the boys put on their rubber boots and went out to the Pond. They couldn't get quite as near it as usual, for the edge was almost at the Ducks' house now, and not so very far from the house of the White Wyandottes, who seemed to think the end of the world had come, and looked very sad with their draggled feathers.

For a little while the boys threw sticks in the water. When the dogs had fetched the sticks they would shake the water from their coats and over the boys, just like shower baths. It was all very jolly, and I don't know which the children enjoyed more, throwing the sticks or the nice cool showers.

But after a while they tired of this, too, and walked up

Robert Gordon Anderson

the pasture to see the Brook.

There it was, racing and romping and tearing along for dear life. It wasn't clear and silvery now, but muddy and brown as if a thousand cups of coffee had been spilled in it. And on it floated many strange things, - branches of trees and a fence-rail, the roof of a pig-pen, an old shoe, and one poor drowned sheep.

"Maybe," said Jehosophat, "maybe, if we watch long enough, some pirates'll come sailin' along with big hats an' swords an' -"

"An' knives in their mouths," Marmaduke suggested.

"But that's not the best thing," Jehosophat went on, "they'll have a flag with a skull an' dead men's bones painted on it."

"Crackey!" exclaimed his brother, just like the big boys. It was a fine word, too, but only to be used on special occasions. And pirates and skulls and dead men's bones certainly made a "special occasion."

Jehosophat seemed to think so, too, for he was singing in high glee,

"Yo, ho, ho,
And a bottle of bay rum."

As these last dread words died on the air, they thought they heard a sound behind them. It was something like a laugh - more, perhaps, like a chuckle. They turned and saw nothing but the high board fence of the cowyard, and, over by the barn, the Toyman, walking very swiftly towards his workshop. Now usually they would have wondered about that; tried to guess what he "would make," but this morning there were other, very grave, things taking their attention.

"Guess it was pirates - ssshhh!" whispered Jehosophat, "they may have disbarked an' be hidin' in the bushes."

But a way of escape was open. It was coming down the stream.

Jehosophat spied it.

"The very thing!" he cried.

It was a big gate which had been carried off by the flood; and it was tossed first to this side and then to the other by the brown water.

"I hope it catches on something an' stops," cried Marmaduke. And they hurried down the Brook towards the Pond. They had to walk pretty fast, too, almost run, to keep up with the gate.

Jehosophat looked ahead.

"Those big roots of the walnut tree might stop it," he said.

And sure enough the gate was caught by the roots and swung in under the branches. The water was more quiet here than out in the stream and it made a fine harbor for the ship. For, you see, after all, it was not a gate but a *ship*!

But they must make sure of their prize. So Jehosophat ran to the barn and fetched some rope. With this he made the ship fast to the trunk of the tree, that is, to the wharf in Walnut Harbour.

But there was more work to be done, for the ship had been damaged by the storm.

"You stand watch an' keep off all pirates," ordered Jehosophat. "I'll be back in three shakes of a lamb's tail."

It was rather a scary thing to stand guard all alone with pirates around, but Marmaduke stuck by the ship and Jehosophat went on his errand.

As he entered the door, the Toyman hid something, quite hurriedly, under a sack. Now that was very mysterious, but the messenger only said to himself, "Guess he's making something for my birthday," then asked aloud, -

"Please, may I have some boards and some nails?"

"To be sure, Mr. Ship's Carpenter."

It was fine to be called that, though Jehosophat wondered how the Toyman knew what he was, when they hadn't told a soul. But then the Toyman knew most everything, all their plans as soon as made.

It didn't take long to mend that ship. Soon the boards were nailed across and the deck was ready for the crew.

"All aboard!" shouted Jehosophat, and then even more loudly, -

"All ashore that's goin' ashore!"

Having said this very splendidly, he turned to his brother.

"I'm Captain Kidd," he told him.

"And what's me?" shouted back Marmaduke excitedly, and excitement is always bad for grammar.

"Oh, you! You're my slave," his brother informed him - in a very grand manner.

This didn't seem to suit Marmaduke, and he tried hard to remember a name Reddy Toms had told him, out of a book of Reddy's, all about pirates and things. But he couldn't think of it at all.

Just then a voice shouted, -

"What ho, Dick Deadeye!"

It was the Toyman, who had been standing in the doorway watching them.

"Dick Deadeye - whew!" Marmaduke rolled the name under his tongue like something that tasted very nice. He was completely satisfied now.

Then something still nicer happened, for, when their backs were turned, something whistled through the air and fell at their feet. Real swords! One for each of them! Now we said they were *real* swords, and they were, though they were made of wood. They could do a lot of damage. The pirates would find that out soon enough. And there was a flag, too, with bones and a skull on it, just as Jehosophat had said.

"Why, it's the Jolly Roger," he told his brother, "that's what they call this flag."

But where did they come from? Marmaduke sort of suspected the Toyman, but he had disappeared, and Jehosophat said, -

"They must have dropped from Heaven an' were sent us to 'venge the people the pirates have killed. It's a sign. Guess we're not pirates after all, but just good sailors an' we'll scrunch those pirates."

Then he thought for a moment.

"But I guess we'll keep this flag anyway, even if it is the pirates'."

And they kept their names as well. They were far too fine to give up.

But just as they were about to go aboard, the Toyman came to the shore.

"What ho!" he said, then again, "what ho!"

That sounded exciting - not like a game at all, but like real life! And he was "saying some more," -

"Avast, me hearties, what's in the wind?"

This last was a very odd question, for whatever could be in the wind, when you can see right through it and it can't hold anything at all. Strange talk it was, to be sure, and the neighbors would never have understood it. Still, folks never understood the Toyman and his language anyway, but *they* did, and Marmaduke called, - "Come 'n, Toyman," when Captain Kidd corrected him.

"Pshaw! That's not the way to say it. You just listen to me."

Then he raised his hands to his mouth like a trumpet and called, -

"Ho, there, you landlubber, will you ship with us?"

The Toyman touched his hat.

"Thankee kindly, Cap'n, but I've killed many a pirate in my time. Now it's *your* chance. But it's blowin' great guns an' ye'd better cruise near shore."

"Ay, ay, sir," shouted the captain as a last farewell, then they set sail. They made quite a voyage of it and had some trouble, for the waves were rough and the seas were high, but they reached port safely at last.

They hadn't seen anything of the pirates yet, and they decided to make another try for it when Hepzebiah came to the wharf. She wanted to sail too, but the Captain only said, very thoughtfully, -

"It's not safe for the women an' children."

However, she cried so hard that they just had to let her on board.

"But if you come, you'll have to be my slave," the Captain told her.

Perhaps that is the reason why he let her sail at all. He wanted a slave very much and since Marmaduke wouldn't be one and was Dick Deadeye anyway, why, the little girl would have to do. Still she didn't care what she was called as long as she could sail on that fine ship.

So they sailed and they sailed, the white flag with the skull and the dead men's bones floating merrily in the breeze. And at last Dick Deadeye called, -

"Cracky! Look where we are! You'd better go back. Remember what the Toyman told us."

But Captain Jehosophat Kidd knew better.

"Pshaw! It isn't deep at all. It wouldn't drown a rat - not even a little mouse."

Then there *was* trouble.

They heard shouts along the shore, and, looking back, saw Fatty Hamm, Reddy Toms, and Sammy Soapstone, jumping around like wild Indians. They looked again - sharply this time - and saw that it wasn't boys after all, but pirates, wicked, cruel, bloodthirsty pirates! And that was bad enough!

"They're trying to capture us," shouted brave Captain Kidd, then, forgetting that his ship was a full-rigged ship and went by sail, he called,

   "Row, brothers, row,
   The stream runs fast."

You see, he remembered that from a poetry book he

had read once and thought it would just suit.

And all the time the crew of the "Jolly Roger" looked angrily back at shore.

"Splash!"

A big stone fell near them. No, it wasn't a stone. It was a - cannon ball! The pirates on shore were trying to knock holes in their ship!

"You're awful shots," the Captain jeered fearlessly. "We're coming ashore to capture your cannon." He was very brave through all these trying times - and so were the crew. And they just turned their ship around and headed straight for the shore, though the cannon balls fell all around them.

But now a more terrible danger threatened. For the rascals on shore had seized long poles and were reaching out over the water, trying to smash holes in the ship, to stove in its hull.

"They're grapplin' irons and marlin spikes," explained the Captain, "and very terrible weapons." He must have been right, for he knew the ways of the sea.

Meantime the ship was beginning to rock. The crew looked around for rescue, but none was in sight.

"We'll sink your ole ship," shouted Pirate Fatty. "You're awful sailors."

And all the time, up and down, and down and up, went the poor little ship. Would they drown? Far off, Dick Deadeye saw the Toyman running, running as fast as he could towards shore. And Rover, too. He was barking for all he was worth, seeming to think it fun. But Rover was only a dog, and couldn't realize the danger at all.

At last the big fat pirate's pole hit the ship a terrible crack, and overboard Slave Hepzebiah fell.

Dick Deadeye reached for her, but his hand only touched her uniform, and over he fell, too, down in the coffee-colored waves.

It was way over his head. Down, down, he sank. He was terribly frightened, with water all around him and in his eyes and his nose and mouth. He was choking, but all he thought of, even then, was his little sister, the poor slave.

The first thing he knew, he felt a strong hand on his shoulder and heard the Toyman's voice saying, -

"Hold on, Sonny, you're all right - just grab on to me."

He had always liked to be held close in the Toyman's arms, especially at night before the fire when he told them stories, but never had those arms felt as safe as now.

Then, all-of-a-sudden he thought -!

"Stop!" he tried to shout, but his mouth was almost too full of water to say anything, "get - bllllllloooo - Hep-ze-bbblllllooo" - and then he had to stop.

But the Toyman laughed as he pulled him safe on the shore.

"Look there," he said.

And Marmaduke did look, and there was Rover dragging his little sister out of the sea by the back of her dress.

The Toyman patted the brave dog on the head.

"He's the hero," he said, "good old Rover!"

Then something fine happened. At least Marmaduke and Jehosophat thought so. And we'll leave it to you to decide whether it was fine or not.

Now the pirates had started to run, but their chief, the big fat one, just before he reached the road, slipped in the mud. And down over the banks into the sea he fell, and the Toyman didn't trouble to fish him out, either. Of course, it wasn't very deep, but Fatty tumbled flat on his back, and the water covered him - all but his stomach, which stuck out above the water like the fat rump of a whale. He got up at last. And a pretty sight he was, not like a bold pirate, but a great big "booby," Mother said, with the mud all over his clothes, and the water going slippity slop in his shoes, and he shouting, "Bbbbbblllllllllloooooooooo - splutter - gerchoo!" worse even than Marmaduke.

Quick as a wink the Toyman lifted Marmaduke on one shoulder, the little girl on the other, as he always carried them, and took them into the house.

And soon their clothes were off, and dry ones on, and - best of all - some nice warm lemonade was trickling down just where the muddy water had been - down the Red Lane.

Robert Gordon Anderson

He felt greatly contented, did Marmaduke, for hadn't they beaten the "ol' pirates," and driven them away? And after that they had heaped coals of fire on their heads, as the minister used to say. Yes sir, they invited the big, fat chief of the pirates into their kitchen, though he didn't deserve it, and gave him some dry clothes, too, though he didn't deserve that, either, and some lemonade into the bargain.

Altogether, it was a very successful day.

IV

THE BLUE CROAKER, THE BRIGHT AGATE,
AND THE LITTLE GRAY MIG

It is odd about Grownups - how mistaken they can be, how sadly mistaken. Now for instance, they *will* insist there are only four seasons when, as every one who has lived in Boyland knows, there are scores more than that.

There's

Sled-time;
Ball-time;
Marble-time;
Top-time;
Kite-time;
Garden-time;
Hay-time;
Harvest-time;
Grape-time;
Nut-time;
Pumpkin-Pie-time;
and
a time
for

Hunting strawberries, elderberries, or red rasps; for

orioles to move, for shad to run, and to go bobbin' for eels; and a whole lot of other famous seasons as well, all happy ones, and too many to count, at least on one set of fingers and toes.

Any American boy will tell you this and - what is more to the point - prove it, too. And so can the Toyman, for, though he is six feet tall, and wears suspenders and long pants, and shaves and all that, he can get down on his knees in the good old brown earth and cry, "Knuckles down!," with the youngest.

Well, then, it was - not Spring, as the grownups would say - but Marble-time - midway between Kite-time and the Time for Red Strawberries, which comes in June.

One day, at the very beginning of this sunny season, the Toyman came back from town. And as usual the children gathered around him. There was no delay, no dilly-dallying, as there was when kindlings were called for. It was funny to see how quickly they *could* gather when they heard the wheels come up the drive. Somehow their particular creak was different from that of any other wheels - and the children could tell it long before ever the wagon came in sight.

When they were younger, the children used to ask a question just as the reins fell over the dashboard and the Toyman jumped to the ground.

"What have you got for me, Toyman?" it always was.

But not now, for Mother had explained it was very bad manners. And Jehosophat and Marmaduke were trying hard to be "Little Gentlemen," and to show Hepzebiah a "Good Example."

Of course, just as Mother had expected, when she suggested all this, Marmaduke asked, -

"But how can a *girl* be a Little Gentleman?"

Mother made it clear.

"Well hardly," she said, "we wouldn't want her to be just that, but by being a Little Gentleman you can teach her to be a Little Lady."

It was hard sometimes, and once in a while the boys didn't think the Little Gentleman game quite so attractive. However, they remembered it pretty well, considering. And today they didn't ask any rude questions, but just waited, though they danced on their toes.

This time he led them all into the kitchen without saying a word.

And then!!! - one after another he took from his pockets little round things - marbles, of course, of all sorts and sizes and colors.

"My!" exclaimed Marmaduke, "there's most a hundred."

And there was, sixty, to be exact. Twenty-seven little ones, colored like clay; six big ones of brown, with spots on them like the dapplings on horses; and six of blue dappled the same way; nine big glass ones with pink and blue streaks like the colorings in Mother's marble cake; nine made of china; and three - one for each - of the beautiful agates - one of dark red and cream, one dark blue and cream, and one that was

Robert Gordon Anderson

mostly pink.

"Now," said Mother, when he had tumbled all the beautiful marbles out on the table, "you've got me in trouble, Frank."

But she didn't mean that. No, indeed. It was all said in fun. They said so many things in fun in the White House with the Green Blinds by the Side of the Road. So she got out her needle and thread, some pieces of flannel, and began.

She made three little bags, each with draw strings. On one she sewed a red J; on the second a blue M; on the third a pink H. You can probably guess for whom each was meant.

By this time it was too dark to see. Mother lit the lamp and started supper. And of course they ate it - they seldom skipped that of their own free will - but after it was over, the Toyman kneeled down on the floor, and Father got down on the floor, too, and they played marbles on the rag rug.

That was pretty nice and interesting, but they looked forward to the real game in the morning, for the real game must be played, not on a rug, but on the good brown earth.

Again the Toyman took a little, oh, just a little time from his work - that is, he meant to, but it turned out a longer "spell" than he had intended.

First they sorted the marbles. And when the sorting was over, each had nine of the little gray ones, which the Toyman told them were called "Migs"; two of the dappled brown ones which he said were "Croakers"; and two of the blue; three "Chineys"; three "Glasseys" with the pink and blue streaks; and one each of the most beautiful of all, - the agates. The blue and cream-colored agate Marmaduke took to match the blue M on his bag; Jehosophat the reddest one to match his letter J; and Hepzebiah the agate that looked most like a strawberry - almost pink it was, like her letter H.

These last beautiful ones, their old friend informed them, were agates, but had other names.

"They called them 'Pures' when I was a boy," he remarked, "but in some places they called 'em 'Reals,' just as in some cities they say pink is for boys and blue for girls, and in some the other way round."

And don't let any one tell you this question of "Reals" and "Pures" isn't important, for it is, surely as much so as "hazards" and "simple honors" which the grownups are forever discussing. In fact this matter of "Reals" and "Pures" was one that had to be settled at once. And Jehosophat settled it.

"I guess," he said, after grave deliberation, "if you called them 'Pures' when you were a boy, we'll call 'em that too."

Now this suggested a question to Marmaduke.

"Say, Toyman, when did you stop being a boy?"

And the Toyman just laughed his hearty laugh and slapped his knees with his rough brown hand. His answer was strange yet very true.

"Tomorrow," he replied.

It was true, you see, for, as they say in school, "Tomorrow never comes," and that is just when the Toyman will stop being a boy.

Meanwhile he was making a ring in the ground, two feet across. In the middle he scooped out a little hole with his heel.

Each put some marbles in the centre, the same number from each bag, and they began. Of course, as you know, they had to stand on the outside of the ring and shoot at the marbles in the hole, that is, they did in that year, in that particular part of the country, though wise men who have travelled much say the rules differ in other states and are changing from day to day.

When anyone put his foot over the line the Toyman would stop him sternly.

"No matter what's the game," he told them, "always play fair."

He showed them the best way to shoot, not by placing the marble in the hollow of the first finger and shooting it out with the thumb, but on the *tip* of the first finger and letting it fly with the thumb.

Now this is of the greatest importance, so always remember it.

However, Hepzebiah couldn't follow that style, so they let her roll her marbles. But the boys were patient and tried again and again until they had learned the right way. They did finely, too - though naturally not as well as the Toyman. They had lent him some of their marbles, and my! wasn't he a fine shot! He would send those marbles flying from their hole like little smithereens in all directions. However, he said the boys were learning fast and would soon catch up with him.

And in a few minutes, strange to say, the Toyman wasn't doing so well - though, maybe - between you and me - he was just giving the boys a chance.

Anyway, before long, the Toyman's pile was growing less and less, while Marmaduke had nine gray marbles - we should say "migs" - one "chiney," two brown "croakers," one blue "croaker," and one "glassey," and his shooter, the "pure," of course. And Jehosophat had ten "migs," two "chimneys," one "glassey," two brown "croakers," and one blue one, and his shooter. But poor little Hepzebiah had only three, counting all kinds. She began to cry, and rubbed her eyes with her two fists. But when, after a little, she stopped and looked down, why she had more marbles than *any* of the players.

I'll tell you a secret, if you won't tell it to a soul - for that wouldn't be fair to Marmaduke and Jehosophat, who were trying their best not to let their right hands know what their left ones were doing.

Well then, if you won't tell, - when Hepzebiah put her two fists to her eyes, quick as a wink the Toyman placed three of his marbles in her pile, and when Marmaduke saw him do that, why he put in four, and Jehosophat, not to be outdone, slipped in five.

"Better than slipping duck's eggs under the old hen, isn't it?" whispered Jehosophat to his brother, who agreed with a nod.

And that is the way the little girl came to win the game.

And so all through marble time they played many games, some of them very close, too, and a few even ties.

However, on one occasion the game didn't turn out so well. That was the time when Fatty Hamm strolled into the yard.

"Hello!" he said, and something chinked in his pockets. It sounded like marbles.

"Hello!" called the boys, not very cordially, for they were always a little suspicious when Fatty happened around.

"Playin' marbles?" he asked.

"Yes," said the two brothers.

"I can beat you," he declared.

"You can't, either," Marmaduke started to yell, but Jehosophat, who was having one of his good days, said, -

"Let's treat him politely. He's mean, but he's company."

"Play 'for fair'?" Fatty next asked.

"Course," replied Jehosophat, "what did you think?"

This friendly state of affairs didn't last very long.

"You're cheating," called Jehosophat a little later.

"I'm not, neither," Fatty shouted very angrily and ungrammatically.

"You are, too," insisted Jehosophat. "The Toyman says you mustn't get over the marbles that way or put your foot in the ring. You've got to 'knuckles down.' Beside you call' slippseys' every time you make a bad shot."

When that strange game was over Fatty had forty-two marbles and they had only nine apiece. Altogether it was very unsatisfactory.

Then something very surprising happened.

Fatty counted the forty-two very carefully, then put them in his bag.

"Here," said Jehosophat, "what are you doing?"

"I won 'em, they're mine," and still Fatty kept putting them in his bag. Marmaduke could hear them dropping in. "Chink, chink," they went, but their "chink, chink" didn't sound so pretty or so much like music as when they were dropping in his own bag.

"That's not the way the Toyman plays," Jehosophat insisted, "when we're through we divide 'em up again so's to be even."

"Your ole Toyman doesn't know everything," Fatty said with a sneer.

And, angry at this, both the brothers shouted, -

"He does, too - he knows most everything there is to know."

But Fatty decided things once and for all.

"Anyway," he declared, "this game's not 'in fun.' You said you'd play 'for fair' and that means 'for keeps.'"

Jehosophat was silent. He hadn't understood what 'for fair' had meant at all. Still, he had agreed to play that way, and so, though he wanted to punch Fatty's head for him, he supposed he'd have to take his losses like a gentleman.

But now Fatty was taking something out of his pocket, something made of wood and shaped like a bridge or a saw with teeth in it. He placed it on the ground.

"Your turn, Joshy," he said.

"What'll I do?" asked Jehosophat.

"Just roll your marbles under this bridge, and if they go through the little holes, you can keep 'em. If they don't, they're mine."

The two boys didn't see through the trick, and very foolishly they thought they might win some of their beautiful marbles back.

So they rolled marble after marble against that little wooden bridge. But it was much harder to aim straight than they had expected. More marbles would hit against the wood and bounce back than ever went through the little holes. And when this strange new game was ended Fatty had fifty-two marbles and they each had four!

Then Fatty walked off.

"Nice game," he said, "I'll come tomorrow."

But the boys didn't second that or give him any warm invitation like saying, "yes, and stay a week." They spoke never a word - just looked and listened - looked at the few marbles left in their own hands, and listened to the "chink, chink, chink" of Fatty's pockets as he walked down the drive.

They were very solemn around the table that night, and though Mother knew there must be something the matter, she didn't ask any questions yet. However, Marmaduke kept reaching down into his pockets so often, to feel the lonely little marbles he had left, - the one agate, and the croaker, and the little gray mig, and the clink of them sounded so weak and thin and lonesome that Father said, -

"Well, how did the game go today?"

"F-f-f-fine," said Marmaduke, but his lip quivered.

Then they knew there surely must be something the matter, and Marmaduke couldn't help saying, -

"That ole Fatty Hamm said he was playing 'for keeps,' and he took away almost all our marbles."

"Humph!" exclaimed Father, and Mother looked at him with an odd look.

"I'm sorry it happened," she said, "but I'm glad, too."

Jehosophat exclaimed:

"Glad we lost our marbles?"

"Not exactly, dear, but I knew it would happen. You see, as the Toyman said, it's always kinder and more fun, too, to play games 'in fun.' If you play anything 'for keeps,' the one who loses is always hurt and feels badly. Supposing you had played with Johnny Cricket, now, and had won all his marbles - how would you feel?"

She didn't need to say any more. They understood.

But after supper the Toyman called the boys into the woodshed. They sneaked out quietly and he whispered to them, -

"Just wait till tomorrow."

"What's going to happen tomorrow?"

And the Toyman gave that old answer of his which was so like him, -

"Wait an' see."

Well, the Toyman had to go to town "tomorrow," which was much sooner than he had expected earlier in the week. And when he came back his pockets chinked right merrily. They were as full of marbles as on his first trip back from town.

They were very beautiful, too, but somehow Marmaduke loved the first blue croaker and the bright agate and the little gray mig best of all.

V

THE OLD WOMAN WHO LIVED ON THE CANAL

In front of the White House with the Green Blinds by the Side of the Road was the Canal; and beyond the Canal the River. They always flowed along side by side, and Marmaduke thought they were like two brothers. The Canal was the older brother, it was always so sure and steady and ready for work. It flowed steadily and evenly and carried the big canal-boats down to the Sea. The River also flowed towards the Sea, but it wasn't at all steady, and never quiet. It was indeed like the younger brother, ever ready for play, although, as a matter of fact, it had been there long before the Canal had been even thought of by the men who built it. But thousands of years couldn't make that River grow old. It was full of frolicsome ripples that gleamed in the sun, and of rapids and waterfalls. Here it would flow swiftly, and there almost stop as if it wanted to fall asleep. And every once in a while it would dart swiftly like small boys or dogs chasing butterflies. Sometimes it would leap over the stones or, at the dam, tumble headlong in sheets of silver.

Little fish and big loved to play in its waters. Of course they swam in the Canal too, but life was lazier there and the fish, like Marmaduke, seemed to prefer the River. There were pickerel and trout and catfish and

Robert Gordon Anderson

eels, and in the Spring the great shad would come in from the Sea and journey up to the still cool pools to hatch out their millions of children.

They looked very inviting this morning, the River and the Canal, and Marmaduke decided he would take a stroll. He whistled to Wienerwurst, who was always the best company in the world, and the little dog came leaping and barking and wagging his tail, glad to be alive and about in such lovely weather, and on they went by the side of the Canal.

They went along very slowly, for it is a mistake to walk too fast on a Spring morning - one misses so many things.

Now and then a big fish would leap out of the River, it felt so gay, and in the little harbours under the banks of the Canal the scuttle-bugs went skimming, skimming, like swift little tugboats at play. In the fields on the other side of the road a meadowlark sang; swallows twittered overhead; and in the grass at his feet the dandelions glowed like the round gold shields of a million soldiers. Yes, altogether it was a wonderful day.

Marmaduke picked a great bouquet of the dandelions - for Mother - then he looked up the towpath. He could see the Red Schoolhouse, and, not so far away, the Lock of the Canal. He was very glad it was Saturday. It was far too nice to stay indoors.

Just then he had a great piece of good luck, for a big boat came by, a canal-boat, shaped like a long wooden shoe. It had no sails and no smokestacks, either, so it had no engine to make it go. It was drawn by two mules who walked on shore quite a distance ahead of it. A long thick rope stretched from the collars of the mules to the bow of the boat. A little boy walked behind the mules, yelling to them and now and then poking them with a long pole to make them go faster. My! how they pulled and tugged on that rope! They had to, for it was a pretty big load, that boat. And it had a big hole in it laden with black shiny coal - tons and tons of it!

Just behind the coal was a clothes-line with scores of little skirts and pairs of pants on it, and behind that, a little house with many children running in and out of the door. A round fat rosy woman with great big arms was calling to the children to "take care," and a man stood at the stern with his hand on the tiller. He had a red shirt on and in his mouth a pipe which Marmaduke could smell a long way off.

The little boy waited until the stern came by so he could see the name of the boat. There it was now, painted in big letters, right under the tiller. He spelled it out, first "Mary," then "Ellen" - "Mary Ellen -" a pretty name, he thought.

The Man With the Red Shirt and the Pipe, and the Round Fat Rosy Woman With the Big Arms, and all the children waved their hands to Marmaduke and he waved back, then hurried ahead, Wienerwurst trotting alongside, to catch up with the boy who was driving the mules.

"'Llo!" said he to the boy, but the boy paid no attention at all, just "licked up" his mules. But Marmaduke didn't mind this rudeness. He thought that probably the boy was too busy to be sociable, and he trotted along

Robert Gordon Anderson

with the mules and watched their long funny ears go wiggle-waggle when a fly buzzed near them. But they never paused or stopped, no matter what annoyed them, but just tugged and strained in their collars, pulling the long rope that pulled the boat that carried the coal that would make somebody's fire to cook somebody's supper some day down by the Sea.

For a long time Marmaduke trotted alongside the boy and the mules, not realizing at all how far he had come. Once or twice he looked back at the "Mary Ellen" and the Man With the Red Shirt and the Pipe, and the little house on the deck. He wished he could go on board and steer the "Mary Ellen," and play in that little house, it looked so cute. The Round Fat Rosy Woman was coming out of it now with a pan of water which she threw in the Canal; and the little children were running all over the deck, almost tumbling in the water.

After quite a journey they drew near the Lock, a great place in the Canal like a harbour, with two pairs of gates, as high as a house, at each end, to keep the water in the Lock.

Outside one pair of gates the water was low; outside the others, which were near him, the water was high; and Marmaduke knew well what those great gates would do. The pair at the end where the water was high would open and the canalboat would float in the Lock and rest there for a while like a ship in harbour. Then those gates would shut tight, and the man who tended the Lock would open the gates at the end where the water was low. And the water would rush out and go down, down in the Lock, carrying the boat with it until it was on a level with the low part of the Canal.

And the boat at last would float out of the harbour of the Lock and away on its journey to the Sea.

But all this hadn't happened yet. There was much work to be done before all was ready.

Now the boat had stopped in front of the high pair of gates. The Man With the Red Shirt and the Pipe shouted to the boy who drove the mules, without taking the pipe out of his mouth. The great towrope was untied and the mules rested while the man who tended the Lock swung the high gates open with some machinery that creaked in a funny way, and the "Mary Ellen" glided in the harbour of the Lock.

Then the man who tended the Lock went to the gates at the lower end. There were more shouts and those gates opened too. The water rushed out of the Lock into the lower part of the Canal, and down, down, went the boat. And down, down, went the deck and the little house on it, and down, down, went the Man With the Red Shirt and the Pipe, and the Round Fat Rosy Woman With the Great Arms, and all the children. Marmaduke started to count them. He couldn't have done that before, they ran around too fast. But now they stood still, watching the water fall and their boat as it sank. Yes, there were thirteen - he counted twice to make sure.

Now the boat had sunk so low that Marmaduke was afraid it would disappear forever, with all the children on it. But there was no danger, for when the water in the Lock was even with the water on the lower side of the Canal it stopped falling, and the "Mary Ellen" stopped, too. At least, there was no danger for the children, but there was for Master Marmaduke, he had

Robert Gordon Anderson

leaned over so far, watching that boat go down, down, down.

All-of-a-sudden there was a splash. It was certainly to be expected that one of the thirteen children had fallen in, but no! - It - was - Marmaduke!

Down, down, down, he sank in the gurgly brown water. Then he came up, spluttering and choking.

"Help, help!" he cried.

Then under he went again.

But the Round Fat Rosy Woman had seen him.

"Quick, Hiram!" she shouted to her husband in a voice that sounded like a man's, "there's a boy fallen overboard!"

"Where?" asked the man at the tiller, still keeping the pipe in his mouth.

She pointed into the brown water.

"Right there - there's where he went down."

Perhaps the Man With the Red Shirt and the Pipe was so used to having his children fall into the coal, or the Canal, or something, that he didn't think it was a serious matter, for he came to the side of the "Mary Ellen" very slowly, just as Marmaduke was coming up for the third time.

And that is a very important time, for, they say, if you go down after that you won't come up 'til you're dead.

Whether it was true or not, Marmaduke didn't know, for he had never been drowned before, and no one who had, had ever come back to tell him about it. Anyway, he wasn't thinking much, only throwing his arms around in the water, trying vainly to keep afloat.

The Round Fat Rosy Woman grew quite excited, as well she might, and she shouted again to the Man With the Red Shirt and the Pipe:

"Don't stand there like a wooden Injun in front of a cigar-store. Hustle or the boy'll drown!"

Then he seemed to wake up, for he ran to the gunwale of the boat, and he jumped over with his shoes and all his clothes on. And, strange to say, he still kept that pipe in his mouth. However, that didn't matter so very much, for he grabbed Marmaduke by the collar with one hand and swam towards the "Mary Ellen" with the other. The woman threw a rope over the side; he grasped it with his free hand, and the woman drew them up - she certainly was strong - and in the shake of a little jiffy they were standing on board, safe but dripping a thousand little rivers from their clothes on the deck. The man didn't seem to mind that a bit, but was quite disturbed to find that his pipe had gone out.

"Come, Mother," said he to the Round Fat Rosy Woman, "get us some dry duds and a match."

And quick as a wink she hustled them into the little house which they called a cabin, and gave Marmaduke a pair of blue overalls and a little blue jumper which belonged to one of the thirteen children. Of course, she found the right size, with so many to choose from. His own clothes, she hung on the line, with all the little pairs of pants and the skirts, to dry in the breeze.

Then she put the kettle on the cook stove and in another jiffy she was pouring out the tea.

"M - m - m - m," said Marmaduke. He meant to say, - "Make mine 'cambric,' please," for he knew his mother wouldn't have wanted him to take *regular* tea, but his Forty White Horses galloped so he couldn't make himself heard.

"There, little boy," said the Round Fat Rosy Woman, "don't talk. Just wrap yourself in this blanket and drink this down, and you'll feel better."

It did taste good even if it was strong, and it warmed him all the way down under the blue jumper, and the Forty White Horses stopped their galloping, and while the men were hitching the mules up again, and the "Mary Ellen" was drifting through the lower pair of gates out of the Lock, he fell fast asleep.

He must have slept for a whole lot of jiffies. When he woke up at last, he looked around, wondering where he could be, the place looked so strange and so different from his room at home. Then he remembered, - he was far from home, in the little cabin of the "Mary Ellen." It was a cosy place, with all the little beds for the children around the cabin. And these beds were not like the ones he usually slept in. They were little shelves on the wall, two rows of them, one row above the other. It was funny, he thought, to sleep on a shelf, but that was what the thirteen children had to do. He was lying on a shelf himself just then, wrapped in a blanket.

The Round Fat Rosy Woman was bending over the stove. It was a jolly little stove, round and fat and rosy like herself, and it poked its pipe through the house just above his head. In the pot upon it, the potatoes were boiling, boiling away, and the little chips of bacon were curling up in the pan.

Outside, he could see all the little skirts and the little pairs of pants, dancing gaily in the wind. He could hear the children who owned those skirts and pairs of pants running all over the boat. The patter of their feet sounded like raindrops on the deck above him.

They seemed to be forever getting into trouble, those thirteen children, and the Round Fat Rosy Woman was forever running to the door of the little house and shouting to one or the other.

"Take care, Maintop!" she would call to one boy as she pulled him back from falling into the Canal.

"Ho there, Bowsprit!" she would yell to another, as she fished him out of the coal.

They were certainly a great care, those children, and all at once Marmaduke decided he knew who their mother must be. The boat was shaped just like a huge shoe and she surely had so many children she didn't know what to do. Yes, she must be the Old Woman Who Lived in a Shoe, only the shoe must have grown into a canalboat.

He wondered about the funny names she called them.

"Are those their real names?" he asked, as he lay on his little shelf

Robert Gordon Anderson

"Yes," she said, "my husband out there with the pipe was a sailor once, on the deep blue sea. But he had to give it up after he was married, 'cause he couldn't take his family on a ship. We had a lot of trouble finding names for the children started to call 'em Mary and Daniel and such, but the names ran out. So, seeing my husband was so fond of the sea, we decided to call 'em after the parts of a ship, not a canalboat, but the sailing ships that go out to sea - that is, all but Squall.

"Now that's Jib there, driving the mules, and that's Bowsprit - the one all black from the coal. Cutwater's the girl leaning over the stern; Maintop, the one with the three pigtails; and Mizzen, the towhead playing with your dog."

"And what are the names of the rest?" Marmaduke asked, thinking all this very interesting.

"Oh!" she replied. "I'll have to stop and think, there's so many of them. Now there's Bul'ark and Gunnel - they're pretty stout; the twins, Anchor and Chain; Squall, the crybaby; Block, the fattest of all; Topmast, the tallest and thinnest; and Stern, the littlest. He came last, so we named him that, seeing it's the last part of a ship.

"Now, let me think - have I got 'em all?" and she counted on her fingers, - "Jib, Bowsprit, Cutwater, Maintop, Mizzen, Bul'ark, Gunnel, Anchor, Chain, Block, Squall, Topmast, and Stern. Yes, that surely makes thirteen, doesn't it? I'm always proud when I can remember 'em."

By this time the potatoes and the bacon and coffee seemed about ready, so she went out on deck, and

Marmaduke slid off his little shelf bed and followed her to see where she was going. On deck was a great bar of iron with another beside it. She took up one bar of iron and with it struck the other - twelve times. The blows sounded way out over the Canal and over the fields and far away, like a mighty fire-alarm, and all the children, that is all but Jib, who was driving the mules and would get his dinner later, came running into the cabin.

A great clatter of tin plates and knives and forks there was, and very nice did those potatoes and that bacon taste.

And it didn't take long for them to finish that meal, either. Then they went out on deck.

The mules were pulling and pulling, and the boat was sailing on and on towards the Sea. They passed by so many places - lots of houses and lots of farms, the Red Schoolhouse and Reddy Toms' house, and Sammy Soapstone's, and the funny place where Fatty lived, and the pigs, fat like himself, ran all over the yard.

Fatty and Sammy were playing on the shore at that very moment. He waved to them and they waved back, but they didn't know they were waving to their old playmate Marmaduke, he was so mixed up with all the children of the woman who lived on the canalboat that looked just like a shoe. How Sammy and Sophy and Fatty would have envied him if they had only known it was he sailing away to the Sea!

But he never arrived there, after all - at least he didn't on that voyage. For, you see, after he had had a wonderful time, running all over the deck with the

Robert Gordon Anderson

thirteen children, and looking down into the big hole where they kept the shiny coal, and exploring the little house on the deck, the Round Fat Rosy Woman and her Husband With the Red Shirt and the Pipe had a talk together.

"We must send him back home," said she, "or his folks'll be scared out of their wits."

The man took a few puffs on his pipe, which always seemed to help him in thinking, then replied,

"We might let him off at the Landing it's up the towpath a piece. We kin find someone to give him a lift."

"That's the best plan," she agreed, "there's the Ruralfree'livery now."

And she pointed to the shore where the horse and wagon of the postman were coming up the road.

"What ho, Hi! Heave to!" she called, raising her hands to her mouth and shouting through them just like a man, "here's a passenger for you, first class."

"Mr. Ruralfree'liv'ry" shook his whip at them, then hollered "Whoa!" and stopped the old horse; and Jib hollered "Whoa!" and stopped his mules, right at the Landing.

Then Marmaduke said "Goodbye." It took him some time, for there was the Man With the Red Shirt and the Pipe; and the Round Fat Rosy Woman; and Jib, Bowsprit, Cutwater, Mizzen, Maintop, Bul'ark, Gunnel, Anchor, Chain, Block, Squall, Topmast, and

Stern; the "Mary Ellen"; and the mules, to say "Goodbye" to. Just before he went ashore the Round Fat Rosy Woman gave him his clothes back, for they were all dry by that time, and she stuffed something in his pocket besides. And what do you think it was? A toy anchor and chain that would just fit the "White Swan," the ship the Toyman had made him.

So he rode home with Mr. Ruralfree'liv'ry and all his sacks of mail. But he kept turning his head for a long while to watch the Man With the Red Shirt and the Pipe, and the Round Fat Rosy Woman, and the Thirteen Children, and all the little pairs of pants that seemed to be waving farewell to him. But soon the "Mary Ellen" drifted out of sight. She was a good boat, the "Mary Ellen."

He almost felt like crying, for he would have liked to have gone on that voyage to see the rest of the world. But, after all, he had seen a great deal of it, and he had that anchor and chain.

VI

TWO O' CAT

It was hard to be called a "kid" - harder still to be left out of the game. And, besides, it wasn't fair. Marmaduke knew he could catch that ball as well, and hit it as often as any of them.

This is the way it began: -

That morning Jehosophat had gone with the Toyman to Sawyer's Mill over on Wally's Creek. Marmaduke felt lonely, for there was nobody but Hepzebiah to play with, and she wouldn't leave her dolls, and he had long ago gotten past playing with *them*. As he was wandering forlornly around the barnyard, wondering what he could do, he heard a shout over by the Miller farm.

"You're out!"

It was a very fascinating cry, an inviting one as well. Looking over the field he saw boys - at least six of them - playing baseball. So he hurried over to get in the game, too.

But his old enemy "Fatty" told him that they didn't "want any *kids* hangin' around."

And Dicky Means agreed with that.

"Naw, we don't want any *kids*!"

"I can catch an' I can pitch - curves, too," Marmaduke protested, but they wouldn't believe him.

"You can't, either," Fatty yelled back, "you'd muff it every time. Wouldn't he, Means?"

He was talking to *Dicky* Means, but he called him by his last name just because he had heard grown-up men do that sometimes and he thought it was very smart.

Again Dicky Means agreed with Fatty.

"*Sure* he'd muff it every time."

Reddy Toms and Harold Skinner didn't take Marmaduke's part, nor did Sammy Soapstone, though he had borrowed Marmaduke's mouth-organ and lost it, and had Marmaduke's appendix all pickled in alcohol in a big bottle and wouldn't give it back, either. But they were all bigger than Marmaduke, so what could he do but sit on the fence and watch them, while his fingers fairly itched to catch one of those "flies." And the crack of the bat against the ball did sound so fine across the field.

At last he couldn't stand it, so he got down from the fence, and shouted at them,

"I wouldn't play in your ole game - not for a *million dollars*!"

And off he walked towards his own barn, swinging his

arms all the way, as if he were holding a bat and showing them just how well he could play. My! what long "flies" he would knock, if he only had the chance - over the dead chestnut tree, over the Gold Rooster on the top of the barn, and even above the Long White Finger of the Church Pointing at the Sky. Maybe, sometime, if he hit it hard enough and just right, the ball would sail on and on, and up and up, to the Moon: and the Ole Man there would catch it and throw it down to him again.

But he would have to practice a lot first, so, when he reached the house, he went in and found a ball of his own. He turned it over and over in his fingers, admiring it. It was a fine one, with leather as white as buckskin but very hard, and thick seams sewed in the cover with heavy thread, winding in and out in horseshoe curves.

It had a dandy name, too, - "Rocket," that was it. And he threw it up high up, up, up, until it reached the eaves of the barn and startled the swallows, who flew out and swept the sky with their pretty wings, chattering angrily at him.

He watched to see where the ball would fall, and ran under it, holding his hands like a little cup. It fell into them, but it fell *out* even quicker than it had fallen in. Jiminy! but that ball was hard! Marmaduke thought the man who made it should have left the "et" from its name and called it plain "Rock" instead. It was just like a rock covered with hard leather.

He tried it again, but he didn't throw it up quite so high.

"Crack!" it went against the side of the barn, and little clouds of hay-dust from the loft danced in the air, and the swallows chattered still more angrily:

"He persists - sists - sists - sists - sists," they called to one another.

This time the ball fell on his cheekbone and raised a lump as round and as hard as a marble.

He didn't cry. Oh, no! for he was trying hard these days to be a regular boy and never to cry even one little whimper. So he just went in the house and Mother put a kiss and some arnica on it - it is always more effective if mixed that way - and out he came and tried it all over again. For regular boys never give up. Of course, at first he threw the ball a little lower than before, but that was only wise. And this time it did fall into his hands and he held it tight. Over and over he practised until his hands were pretty red from catching the hard "Rocket" ball, but he felt very happy inside - which is what counts, for one doesn't mind being sore *outside* if one is all right *within*.

However, all the time he could hear the sound of that bat over on the Miller lot. Then - all of a sudden - he heard an altogether different sort of noise - more like a crash and a smash than a crack.

"Glass!" that was it!

"Hooray!" he shouted in delight, "*now* that Fatty's going to get it."

But he was wrong. Fatty was too plump to hit a ball so hard. It was Dicky Means that had done it. And, like

Fatty, he was always up to tricks, only usually Fatty *planned* them and Dicky *did* them.

Yes, it was Dicky Means who had hit that ball right through Mis' Miller's window, the big parlor window, too, and she expected the Methodist ladies of the Laborforlovesociety that very afternoon. There was Mis' Miller now, running out of the house and shrieking, -

"You younglimbosatan, you'll pay for that!"

"Pleeze, Mis' Miller, I haven't any money," Dicky was saying, very politely, with his eye on the broom she held in her hand, "I'll pay you tomorrow."

"No, you'll settle it _now_," she told him - very cross she was, too, "or I'll tell your mother, and your father'll paddle you in the woodshed." Then she added, - "an' you won't get your ball."

Dicky seemed to be more worried about the ball than about the woodshed, for he whined.

"Aw, pleeze, Mis' Miller, have a heart!"

You see, "Have a heart!" was an expression he had heard down in the city, and for the last week the boys had been using it every chance they got.

Still it didn't work on Mis' Miller, for she only shook her head angrily and took her broom and shouted, -

"Scat, get out!" - just as if they were so many cats - "an' don't come back for the ball till you come with the money in your hand."

And as everybody in the neighborhood used to say, "Gracious, but Mis' Miller has a turrible temper!" or "Whew, but can't she get mad?" and because she was flourishing that broom right in their faces, why, they did scat like so many cats, just as she had told them.

Across the field they all came running, straight towards Marmaduke, who pretended not to see them at all, but just kept passing his Rocket ball from one hand to the other, trying to juggle it like the trick men in the circus.

When they saw that ball, all the boys suddenly grew very polite to Marmaduke.

"Lend us your ball, Marmy!" they said.

"Wouldn't you like to have it!" he replied, still juggling the ball, but he watched them out of the corner of his eye. They had been pretty mean to him, but he supposed he ought to be decent even if they weren't, and besides it would be fine to play a real game with "sides" instead of one just by himself.

"All right," he said, after making them wait long enough to want that ball very much, "if you'll play 'sides' 'stead of' two o' cat,' and let me be captain."

"Aw!" said Dicky, "you're not big enough."

"All right," replied Marmaduke, still juggling that fine Rocket ball, "you'll have to play with some ole rock then."

"Aw, come 'n, have a heart!"

Marmaduke thought it over for a little while. To "have

a heart" was like "heaping coals of fire" on people's heads, in minister's language, he supposed. And he wasn't so fond of that. But anyway he gave in.

"All right," he agreed, "come 'n, where'll we play?"

"Here," said Fatty, "this big rock'll be home-plate, and that one over there by the chestnut tree 'first.' An' we'll choose up sides - first choosin'!"

Then Dicky, who insisted on being the other captain, picked up the bat and threw it with the handle uppermost to Fatty, who caught it around the middle. Then Dicky clasped his fingers around the bat just above Fatty's hand; then Fatty put his left hand above Dicky's right; and Dicky his left hand next; and so on until their fingers almost reached the handle of the bat. There was just a little space left. If Fatty could squeeze his plump fingers in between Dicky's and the top he would win, and he could have first choice of the best players for his side. But his fingers were much too fat.

"Your pinky's over," said Dicky, and Reddy Toms picked up a flat stone and scraped it over the top of the bat, and Fatty howled and let go.

So it was Dicky's turn to choose, and Marmaduke waited breathlessly. He hoped that he would be chosen first, second anyway. He ought to be, for wasn't it his ball they were going to play with!

But -

"I'll take Reddy," said Dicky;

"Sammy," said Fatty;

"Skinny," chose Dicky next;

"Froggy Waters," chose Fatty - and poor little Marmaduke was left to the last, as if he were the worst player in the whole world.

"Well," said Dicky, "I spouse I've *got* to take him. But he'll lose the game for us."

He turned to Marmaduke.

"I'll tell you what, Marmy," he said, "you can be the spectators - a whole pile of them - in the grand stand. Wouldn't you like to be a grand stand? That's great. Isn't it, fellows?"

"Sure," they all said, grinning, but Marmaduke didn't want to be any spectator, not even a grand stand. He wanted to be doing things, not watching. Lose that game, would he? No, he'd show them, he'd win it instead. He'd hit that ball clean over the fence - so far they'd never find it. But whew! That wouldn't do. He'd better not hit it quite so far or he'd lose his dandy Rocket ball.

But they had to give in and let him play before he would give them that ball. Then the two captains told their men to take their positions.

"I'll pitch," declared Dicky, "'n Reddy'll catch. Skinny you play 'first,' and Marmaduke out in the field. You kin go to sleep, too, for all I care - for you can't catch anything even if you had a peach basket to hold it in."

"Play ball!" shouted Fatty, and they all took their places, Dicky's team in the field, and Fatty's at the bat.

Marmaduke had to stand way out, and he didn't have much to do for a while, for the other team either struck out, or hit the ball towards Dicky, the pitcher, or Skinny at 'first.' Once a ball did come his way "Hold it!" shouted Dicky, but Marmaduke was so excited that he threw himself right at it, and the ball rolled between his legs.

"Aw! didn't I tell you?" said Dicky in disgust, and all on the other team shouted:

"Butterfingers!"

And, as every boy in the world knows, it is a great disgrace to be called "Butterfingers."

When the first inning was over the score stood six to five, and Fatty's team was ahead.

In the next inning the ball never once came towards Marmaduke, way out there in the field. All he could do was to watch the other boys catch the "pop-flies," stop the grounders, or run back and forth between first base and home. It was hard, too, when Marmaduke wanted so much to be in the thick of it.

Before long the score stood seventeen to fifteen, still in favor of Fatty's team. At last they were put out, and it was Marmaduke's turn to bat. If he could only knock a home run it would bring Skinny in and tie the score.

"Strike one!" called Sammy, who was catching.

Marmaduke swung at the next one too wildly.

"Strike two!"

And then, sad to tell, -

"Strike three!"

He was out - no doubt about it!

"Aw!" exclaimed Dicky, "what'd I tell you - you ought to be fired."

Marmaduke felt very much ashamed as he took his place out in the field again, with the score thirty-six to thirty against them.

Just then the Toyman and Jehosophat came up the road on their way back from Sawyer's Mill, and the Toyman stopped his horses to watch the game for a minute. Marmaduke gritted his teeth and clenched his hands. He would have to do well now when they were looking on.

Before he knew it, two of the other team were out. Then, all of a sudden, he heard a loud crack. Looking up, he saw the ball sailing through the air. It wasn't sailing towards Dicky or Skinny. It was coming straight in his direction!

He formed his hands in the shape of a cup and waited. He was going to hold that ball - if it ever got there. And, sure enough, it fell in his outstretched hands. My! how that Rocket ball stung and burned! But he hung on for dear life.

"Butterfingers!" he heard Fatty call to "rattle" him. And that settled the matter, for, if he hadn't heard that word, he might have dropped the ball after all, but he was so determined to make Fatty take it all back that he made his fingers tight as a vise around the ball - and it stayed - it stayed there!

When he came in to take his turn at bat, Dicky patted him on the shoulder.

"Good boy, Mary!" he said, and Outfielder Green felt as pleased and proud as before he had been ashamed. But he felt even happier a little later.

It was the last half of the last inning. Reddy and Skinny each made one run and Dicky made two, and now the score stood thirty-six to thirty-five. Fatty's team was only one run ahead, and Dicky was on first with Marmaduke at the bat.

Now was Marmaduke's chance to win the game - the chance of a lifetime!

Fatty twirled the ball in his hand. Though he was fat, he could pitch like a regular pitcher. At least his motions were just as funny. He would curl up his fingers in a strange way to make what he called a curve. Then he would hold the ball up to his chin and look wisely over at first base, watching Dicky. Then he would curl his arms around his head several times, and at last he would let the ball fly.

Marmaduke tried hard to hit it, but he just tipped it.

"Foul!" called the catcher.

And Marmaduke missed the next one and the next. He had only one chance left now. And Fatty twisted himself up almost in knots, to make an extra fine curve, I suppose, for Marmaduke's benefit. Six times he did this before he let the ball go.

It came towards the home-plate and Marmaduke, as fast as an arrow. He gritted his teeth, and gripped his hands tight around the bat, and hit at that Rocket ball harder than he ever had in his life; and all the time his ears were listening for the "crack!"

Of course, it all happened very quickly, more quickly than we can ever tell about it in words, but - to make a long story short - he heard that crack!

He had hit it! And away the Rocket ball flew towards the dead chestnut tree, up, up, by the old crow's nest, and plop! right in the nest it dropped.

And Dicky came racing home, and Marmaduke not far behind him, his face red with excitement and his eyes shining.

And how the team cheered him now, and patted him on the back, and said "Good boy, Mary!" again, and how happy he felt!

There was a nice ending to it too, although the dandy Rocket ball was lost in the old crow's nest. For, when he told them about it all at the supper-table that night, Father turned to the Toyman, and, reaching into his pockets, where some money jingled, said: -

"So the home-team won, did they? though they lost the ball? Well, Frank, there are some more 'dandy Rockets' where that came from, aren't there?"

The Toyman was quite sure there were, and Father added, -

Robert Gordon Anderson

"And that baseball glove, that big catcher's mitt that Marmaduke always wanted - do you 'spouse that's still in the store?"

Again the Toyman seemed rather hopeful, and the promise was fulfilled on the following Saturday. And many a time the hard Rocket ball and lots of other balls, too, thumped in that big leather mitt.

VII

THE FAIRY LAMP

Once in about every so often, it seems, little boys just *have* to get sick. Sometimes it is their own fault; sometimes the fault of the weather; and sometimes there doesn't seem to be any reason at all - except maybe germs. And who ever saw a real live germ walking around, except, perhaps, doctors looking through microscopes? And, besides, germs are too tiny to make a real big boy with pockets in his trousers, and a reader, and a geography, go to bed.

But that is just what had happened to Marmaduke.

He hadn't felt so sick in the daytime - just sort of dreamy, and not like playing at all. He only wanted to lie where he could watch the fingers of the sun-beams stray over the rag rug and pick out the pretty colors in it, and where he could see Mother and call to her when he wanted her. That was always important - to have her near.

At supper all Mother would give him was a cup of warm milk. She said he couldn't have anything solid, not even bread. But after all, perhaps it was better, for his appetite wasn't so very big. He had only asked because he thought he ought to have things Jehosophat had, and didn't want to be deprived of any of his privileges.

Those two round things - like cherries - stuck in his throat so. What was it the doctor called them? Tonsils, that was it. And they felt as big as footballs now, and, oh, so sore!

The doctor decided he had "tonsil-eatus" - a funny name. He called out to Mother to inquire if they would really "eat us" - and how they could "eat us" when they were in your throat already. He felt rather proud of that joke and better for having made it - for a little while, anyway.

There was one "'speshully fine" thing about being sick. Mother would always send Jehosophat and Hepzebiah into the spare room to sleep, and she would come herself and lie down in Jehosophat's bed, right next to the little sick boy, right where he could reach out his hand and place it in hers. That was "most worth" all the aches and the pains.

It was all right to have Father near, but somehow Marmaduke felt better if it was Mother that lay by his side. Her hands and her voice were sort of cool and they drove the bad things that came in his dreams far away.

There was one other fine thing about being sick the Fairy Lamp!

At least that was what the children had named it. It was really a little blue bowl, not light blue like his oatmeal bowl, but almost as blue as periwinkles, or the sky some nights. It had little creases on the outside, "flutings," Mother said, like the pleats in her dress. Inside the bowl was a thick white candle, and it had a curly black wick like a kewpie's topknot.

Now Mother wanted to make sponge for the bread, but Marmaduke pleaded, -

"I want you to stay with me, I feel so sick."

"Wouldn't my little boy let me go - just for five minutes?"

He thought that over for a little while. Then, "Yes," he said slowly, "if you light the Fairy Lamp."

So she struck the match and touched it to the wick. The wick always seemed lazy about being lit. It acted as if the match were waking it up.

But all of a sudden it would burst into flame, and the dark blue of the bowl would turn into light blue - oh, such a pretty color, not like the bluing Hannah put in the water to make the clothes white, nor would it match Sophy Soapstone's electric blue dress. It was more like a blue mist, just such a shade as the fairies would wear.

Marmaduke watched it a long time. Sometimes the little flame sputtered, sometimes it waved in the air, or dipped and bowed in his direction, and once it *actually* winked at him.

From where he lay he could see a bright star shining through the window. He tried to look with one eye at the light and with the other eye at the star, both at the same time. The star seemed sort of blue, too.

"I wonder if the little light is the baby of the star," he said to himself.

And when he looked at the star again, he saw a ray travel down from it into the window, right towards his eyes.

He blinked, and the light grew brighter. It made a pathway reaching from the sky to his bed. Something seemed to be traveling down the bright pathway, singing a song as it came.

First he thought it must be an angel, then a fairy with wings like a moth.

He shut his eyes a minute, to see what would happen, and he heard the voice singing a funny sort of song - no, not funny, but pretty.

And this was the song:

> "Light, light
> By day or night;
> Stars in the skies,
> Stars in the eyes."

He opened his. And there before him, in front of the window, stood a little lady. He thought she was dressed in white, then he decided it was yellow, then gold and white.

She walked, yet she seemed to be pasted on a big, shiny star. The top point rose just above her head, making the peak of a crown. The two middle points stuck out beyond her shoulders like bright moth wings, and the two bottom points extended below her waist, and away from her, like the ends of a sash.

At first Marmaduke thought she must be a painted doll, such as you see in the magazines about Christmas time, made for little children to cut out. But her golden hair was not still like that, but was always in motion like crinkly water that flows over the stones in the brook when the sun shines on it. And there on the rag rug, his own rag rug, were her little feet - very white, with little toes, and she could sing, too. My, how she could sing! No, she was not any painted doll.

She was going on with that song now:

> "Far and near,
> Bright and clear,
> On sky and sea,
> And the Christmas tree."

"'Llo!" said Marmaduke - then he stopped, ashamed. That was the way he talked to the fellows at school. He mustn't speak to such a beautiful lady that way. So - "How do you do?" he corrected himself.

But she only smiled and said - what do you think?

"'Llo! little boy" - just like himself. That seemed to set her singing again: -

> "Low and high,
> In the lake or the sky;
> High and low,
> In the crystal snow."

Then she stopped.

Robert Gordon Anderson

"Is there any more to it?" asked Marmaduke. "Oh, yes, one could go on forever"

"On the church spire,
Or in the fire;
On the wavelet's tip,
Or the mast of a ship;
In the shining gem
Over Bethlehem;
In the little cradle,
With the ox in the stable,
A baby fair
It was brightest there!"

"Now is *that* all of it?" Marmaduke asked her.

"Oh, there's lots more, but I'll sing just the last part for tonight" - and she told him the end:

"And in Mother's eyes,
Just as bright as the skies."

Marmaduke thought she was right in the last part of the song, anyway. Of course, he didn't understand exactly what it was all about, but it was a very pretty song, and he would think it over in the morning. But then his curiosity got the better of him.

"What did you come down here for?"

"Oh, I saw the light in your window," she explained, "and I thought maybe it was a little lost star. You see, we have to look out for them. When we do find a star that has lost its way we take it back -"

"Do you stick it up there with a pin?"

This question seemed to strike her as very amusing, and she laughed. And when she laughed it sounded like church bells far, far off, or the voice of the Brook.

"Oh, no," she said as soon as she could speak. "Do I look as if I could be stuck up there by a pin?"

"No-o-o, but what do you do? Just float around - or swim?"

"Well, that's the way you Earth people would put it - but we have another word for it."

"What is the word?"

She shook her head.

"That I can't tell you, for you'd never understand it, but it's a very pretty word."

Marmaduke sighed.

"I'd like to know it," he said, "but I suppose I can't."

And the Star Lady answered, -

"Not now, perhaps some day."

"Do you do anything else besides hunting for little lost stars?"

"Oh, yes," she said, coming a trifle nearer his bed, "sometimes we find little stars on earth that have never been in the sky, and they shine so very brightly that we take them up there, too."

"What kind of stars?"

"Would you like to see them?"

"You bet I would," Marmaduke started to say, then stopped. That sounded rather rude. Still she didn't reprove him; she didn't seem to mind it a bit. There was something very homelike about her, for all she was so radiant and bright.

"I understand perfectly," she assured him, "but we must be off before daylight." Then she turned to the bureau.

"Take the Little Blue Lamp with you, then you'll seem like a star, too."

Now long ago Marmaduke had made another trip to the skies, to see The Old Man in the Moon, but that journey was never like this. This was so much more beautiful.

He didn't feel as if he were walking or riding, just rising in the air with one hand clasped in the fingers of the Star Lady, the other around the little lamp.

Marmaduke wondered if all the people would look up and see his little light.

"Perhaps they can see just the light and not me," he said to himself, "and that would be just right."

They rose up over the trees, then over the brook, and he saw himself shining in the brook. It looked as if his twin were lying there in the water, and he laughed out loud - that is he thought he did. But he found he wasn't making any sound. Instead of words, sparkles seemed to come from his mouth, like the twinkles of a star.

He asked the Star Lady about that. It was very funny, but now that they were getting up in the clouds he couldn't hear his own voice and she couldn't hear it, either, but they understood each other just the same.

"When a star twinkles, it is laughing," she explained, and it all seemed very clear to him.

Now they passed through great clouds. When they rose above them he looked down. They seemed like white islands in a clear blue sea. And the sky was the sea. It wasn't like water, but just as cool, and the earth, and the towns, and the trees lay like places buried at the bottom of the ocean.

He tried to step on a cloud, and he couldn't feel anything at all under him, yet it didn't give way - he could sit down on it. He did lie down for a little while, it felt so soft and nice, but the Star Lady made him get up.

"We must hurry, for way over there I see the Sun. He's stirring in his sleep, and when he gets up and washes his face -"

"Does he wash his face?" interrupted Marmaduke, "just like real people?"

"Yes, he rubs cloud lather all over it, and then he dips his face in the bowl of the ocean."

"How does he dry it?"

"Oh, the morning wind does that," she replied, smiling at such a parade of questions, "but let's go before he starts to wash up, for I must show you all the star fields. It's only a few steps up."

"But I don't see any steps," exclaimed the little boy.

She smiled.

"Don't you?" she said, "you've been climbing them all the time."

"But it's such a long way to come, and my legs don't feel a bit tired," he persisted, a little doubtfully.

"Oh, no one ever gets tired in the skies," she explained, "we never get tired and we never grow old."

"Do you live forever 'n ever?"

"Yes, forever," she answered gently, "but there are the fields."

Before them and all around them they stretched - as far as his eyes could see, and as far as they could have seen if he had had the biggest telescope in the world.

They were not green like those of Earth, but blue - blue as if each blade of grass were a blade of violet. And each field was thickly planted with bright little gleams like fireflies, winking, winking through the night.

And here and there was a great big star, like the Star Lady herself, walking about - no, it wasn't that - they were *floating* about the meadows. How Marmaduke wished he knew the word she had said they used in the skies for "walking."

"Are they stars or angels?" he asked her.

"Yes and no," she replied. Her answer was very strange, but she wouldn't explain it.

Suddenly Marmaduke thought of a question he had often asked people down on Earth. He could put it to the Star Lady and see if she would give the same answer as Mother. It was an old, old question that little children have asked ever since the world began.

"Who made the stars?" it was.

"God," she answered gently, "at least He made the big ones - but not the little ones."

"And who made them?"

"Oh, the people on earth. Perhaps you made a few yourself," she added.

"*Me*? How ever could I make stars?" And he stared at her in wonder.

"Oh, yes you can. Do you see those little ones there? They are the kind deeds people do on Earth. We go looking for them, and we can find them easily, for they shine out even in the darkest woods and the darkest streets. Then we put them up here. Look hard and perhaps you can find some you recognize."

Marmaduke did look hard. There was one near him. It was very little, but, somehow, as he looked he seemed to know it.

He went very near it. It twinkled like a real star, yet it was round as a bubble. And in it, just as in a soap bubble, he saw a picture.

The Star Lady was looking at him with an amused smile.

"What do you see?" she asked.

Yes, sure enough, there was a picture in it, a little faint, but he could make it out a horse and a bright red cart and on the seat a boy with crutches.

"Why it's Little Geeup and Johnny Cricket!" he exclaimed.

"Yes, it's the picture of the time you took him for a ride," she answered. "I saw you do it, and I went down to Earth, and took that kind, bright little star deed, and planted it here in this very same field."

"Oh, oh!" It was all he could say, it was so wonderful.

Then he saw another field not far away that was full of particularly bright stars.

"I think I know those," he told the Star Lady, "they seem like friends."

"Do they? No wonder!"

Then she looked at him, her head on one side, and a smile in her eyes.

"I won't tell you what they are. I'm going to let *you* tell *me*."

"Oh, I know, I know," he cried, "they're Mother's kind deeds - all she's done for me and Jehosophat and Hepzebiah - and, oh, how many there are!" he added.

"Yes indeed, my dear. You never guessed there were so many, did you?"

Marmaduke grew very solemn as he replied, -

"But I won't forget now *ever*."

From where they stood, the great blue fields rose into a hill. And on the top of the hill was a beautiful star, the largest of all.

"And what is that?" the little boy asked his new friend.

"The star that shone over the cradle in Bethlehem."

He begged her to let him go nearer, but she shook her head.

"Not tonight. Someday you'll see it very clearly."

He was disappointed at that.

"When can I?" he asked.

"I do not know - but someday you and all in the world will see it, when the Earth people are kind to each other - not once in a while, but every day - *all the while* -"

"Anyway," said Marmaduke, "I don't think that star is any prettier than Mother's. It's *bigger* but not *prettier*."

Robert Gordon Anderson

"No, dear," she said, "not any more beautiful - it's all the same light. But the Sun is putting on his gold shoes. Look - over there," she added, "you can see the reflection."

And sure enough, as Marmaduke looked over to the East, the edge of the sky was turning to gold.

"You'll have to say goodbye now," the Star Lady told him, not sadly but gently, "to all the stars and to me. But before you go, listen, and you'll hear them all singing together. They always do, in the morning before the Sun comes. There, can you hear it?"

He listened, oh, so hard, but all he could hear was music like sleigh bells that were very far away.

"I hear something," he told her, "but it isn't clear. It sounds so far, far off."

"Someday you'll hear that clearly, too," she said, then turned. "Goodbye, my dear, I'll look out for your stars again, all the little ones you make each day. Don't forget."

And as he felt himself sinking, he saw the Star Lady waving at him from above, and he was sure she was singing again:

"Light, light
By day or night;
Stars in the skies,
Stars in the eyes."

Again he opened his. There was the Blue Fairy Light winking at him - and his mother's hand was on his forehead. How good it felt! And how cool her voice sounded!

"Was it a nice dream, dear?" she asked him. He didn't answer that question. Instead he said shyly,

"Mother -"

"Yes, dear?"

"Your eyes are like -"

"Like what, my dear little boy?"

"Like stars," he finished drowsily, then fell asleep, her hand still on his forehead.

Robert Gordon Anderson

VIII

THE ANIMALS' BIRTHDAY PARTY

Birthdays are always important events, but some are more important than others. The most important of all, of course, is one you can't remember at all - the zero birthday, when you were born.

After that, the fifth, I suppose, is the red letter day. A boy certainly begins to appreciate life when he gets to be five years old. Next, probably, would come the seventh, for a boy - or a girl - is pretty big by then, and able to do so many things. In old Bible days seven was supposed to be a sacred number, and even today many people think it lucky. Why, at the baseball games the men in the stands rise up in the seventh inning and stretch, they say, to bring victory to the home team.

The seventeenth birthday is the next great event. By that time a boy is quite grown up and ready for college; and on the twenty-first he can vote. But after that people don't think so much of birthdays until their seventieth or so, when they become very proud of them once more. Perhaps they grow like little children again. Wouldn't it be funny to have, say, eighty candles on one cake? But what cook or baker makes cakes big enough for that?

Marmaduke wasn't looking so far ahead. All he was thinking about was his own birthday, which came that fine day, his seventh; and he was wondering if Mother would put the seven candles on his cake, and if it would turn out chocolate, which he very much hoped.

About three o'clock of this same day, Mother looked out of the window and said "Good gracious!," which were the very worst words she ever said; and Father looked up from the cider-press which he was mending, and said "By George!", which were the very worst he ever said; and the Toyman looked up from the sick chicken to which he was giving some medicine, and said "Geewhillikens!" And whether or not that was the worst he ever said I do not know. I hope so.

What could they be exclaiming about? *Marmaduke*! He was all alone as far as human beings went, for Jehosophat was putting axle-grease on his little red cart, and Hepzebiah was playing with Hetty, her rag doll, and the rest were busy at their tasks, as we have just seen.

But he had some fine company, oh, yes, he had. He was giving a birthday party for the animals.

And this is the way he persuaded all his noisy quarrelsome friends of the barnyard to come to his party:

First he went to the barn and filled one pocket - you see, he was a big boy now and had pockets - one, two, three, four, five, six, seven - one over his heart, two close by his belt, one on the inside of his jacket, one on each side of his hips, and two in the back of his corduroy trousers. Well, he filled pocket number one with golden kernels of corn from the sack; pocket number two with meal from another sack; and he filled pocket number three with lettuce leaves from the garden; and number four with birdseed from a little box. That makes four pockets.

To fill the others, he had to make three more journeys - three very strange journeys, so strange you could never guess where he was going. First he went to the wagon-shed, and there, because it was near the three kennels, was kept the box of dog-biscuit. Six of these biscuits went in the fifth pocket. Let's see - yes, that leaves two more to be filled.

For the sixth, he went into his own little room and got a bottle with a stopper in it, one which he had begged from the doctor that time he was sick. Then he went to the springhouse by the well, and filled the little bottle with milk from the big can.

But the seventh pocket had the strangest load of all. He took his shovel and actually dug some worms from the garden, long, wriggly worms - "night-walkers," the boys call them - and placed them in a can, and presto! that too went into his pocket, the seventh. And now all the pockets were filled.

And, mind you, he did all this by himself. And when he came back from all these errands he bulged out in such funny places, the places where he had stuffed his pockets, so that he looked as if he had tremendous warts or knobs all over his body.

"Did you ever!" said Mother, and all three - she, the Toyman, and Father - kept watching, trying hard not to laugh. It paid them to watch him, too, for they were going to see something worth-while, better than a "movie," better even than a circus.

Well, after all the errands were over, Marmaduke collected some shingles, and all the cups and tins in which the Three Happy Children made mud-pies. And he spread them out on the table in the summer-house very carefully.

Can you guess what he did that for? I don't believe you can. I know I couldn't.

Then he took his little scoopnet, and went to the pond and put the net in. Out it came, and in the meshes flopped and tumbled and somersaulted three tiny fish.

These he placed in one of the pans on the table in the summer-house, and then hurried to the rabbit-hutch and opened the sliding door and called, -

"Come, Bunny, Bunny,
An' don't be funny!"

But first we must explain that Marmaduke had a queer trick of making rhymes. I guess he caught it from the Toyman, who used to make lots for the children, just to see them laugh. So Marmaduke got the habit. And making rhymes is just as catching as measles and whooping cough, only it doesn't hurt so much.

Of course, some of Marmaduke's rhymes weren't very good, but he tried his best, which is all you can ask of anybody. Anyway, we will have to tell you them just as he made them, so you can see what sort of a party he had.

So he said, -

"Come, Bunny, Bunny,
An' don't be funny!"

It didn't mean anything much, but he just said it.

And out, hippity hop, hippity hop, came the White Rabbits, making noses at him in the odd way of their kind.

Holding out the lettuce leaves in front of their wriggling noses, he coaxed them over to the summer-house, and when they got there, he placed a leaf in one of the dishes, saving the rest for the feast.

And the Bunnies made funnier noses than ever and nibbled, nibbled away at their plates.

Then he called out loud, -

"Here chick, chick, chick,
Come quick, quick, quick!"

And all the White Wyandottes came running. Mother Wyandotte and all the little ones, and all their relatives, hurrying like fat old women trying to catch the trolley car. Even lordly Father Wyandotte himself stalked along a little faster than usual, and I guess the Big Gold Rooster on the top of the barn tried to fly down too, but he was pinned up there tight on the roof, and so couldn't accept the invitation, much to his grave dissatisfaction.

Marmaduke put only one or two kernels of corn from his first pocket, in the plates for the White Wyandottes, to hold them there until the rest of the guests could come. He wanted to get them all together and make a speech to them, the way Deacon Slithers did when they gave a purse of gold to the minister. He was going to present himself with something at that speech. He had it all planned out, you see.

So next he called the Pretty Pink Pigeons from their house on the top of the barn.

"Coo, coo,
There's some for you."

And the Pretty Pink Pigeons accepted his invitation very quickly, and he tempted them, too, all the way to the summer-house, with a little of the bird-seed from the fourth pocket.

And then he called, -

"Goose, Goose, Goose -"

At first he couldn't think of anything nice for them, but just kept calling, "Goose, Goose, Goose," over and over until he thought up a bright idea - a fine rhyme, -

"You've no excuse."

And then to the Turkey, -

"Turkey, come to my party,
If you don't, you're a smarty."

Sort of silly, wasn't it? - but, no, I guess that was pretty good.

Then he yelled, -

"Here Pussy Cat, Pussy Cat,
You'll have a bite of that."

And -

"Wienie and Brownie and Rover,
Come 'n over, come 'n over, come 'n over!"

And at last, -

"Here, little fish,
Is a nice little dish."

All things considered, he did pretty well, didn't he?

Now he emptied all the different kinds of food, from his seven different pockets, on the little shingles and the little dishes on the table in the summer-house.

There was corn for the White Wyandottes and Mr. Stuckup the Turkey, and some, too, for the Foolish White Geese; and meal for the Pretty Pink Pigeons; and lettuce leaves for the hippity-hop white Bunnies; and milk from the little bottle for the Pussy; and puppy biscuit for the three Dogs; and worms for the Little Fish, all placed very politely in their little dishes.

It was a grand party. No wonder Mother said, "Good gracious!" and "Did you ever!"; and no wonder Father whistled, and said, "By George!", and the Toyman slapped his overalls, and said "Gee-willikens!" - and perhaps a lot of other things besides.

But there was one serious trouble about this party.

Marmaduke couldn't keep sufficient order to make that important speech, which was to have been the event of the celebration.

He stood up on the bench in the summer-house, put his hands in his new pockets, made a fine bow, and began:

"Ladees and gen'lemen an' all others, Mr. Rooster and Mrs. Rooster an' General Turkey" - but he could get no further.

The White Wyandottes were jumping all over the table, and the Pretty Pink Pigeons, who were very tame, were trying to get in his pockets for more of the feast; and Rover and Brownie and Wienerwurst were jumping up and trying to lick his face; and his grand speech turned out something like this:

"Down, Rover! Get away, you crazy Geese! Stop that, Bunny! Stop it, I say - scat!! - scat!!! -"

Well, by this time Wienerwurst was biting the tails of the Pretty Pink Pigeons again; and Brownie was chasing the rabbits; and the Geese were flapping their wings and crying, "hiss, hiss!"; and the Pigeons were flying back to their home on the roof; and Rover had his mouth full of White Geese feathers; and Tabby was swallowing the little fish - and - and - Marmaduke was almost crying.

"I'll take it all back," he yelled, "you're no ladies and gen'lemen you're - you're just mean an' I won't ever ask you to my party again."

Of course, by this time, Mother and the Toyman and Father weren't just standing still and looking and saying things - they were running - and - saying things! - running straight for that party which had turned out such a grand fight.

They tried to save what they could from the wreck. They spanked little Wienerwurst until he let go of the tails of the Pretty Pink Pigeons, and they got the Bunnies safe back in their hutch, and the White Wyandottes in their yard, and Mr. Turkey in his.

But they couldn't save the poor little fish. It was very sad, but it was too late. Tabby wasn't like Jonah's whale. What she had once swallowed she wasn't apt to give up.

Marmaduke felt very much hurt and very indignant about the way he had been treated. As Father said, "it was a grave slight to his hospitality."

However, he forgot all about it when he saw the new skates which Mother and Father had waiting for him, and the grand Noah's Ark which the Toyman had made with his very own hands. There isn't much use telling the colors in which it was painted, because you know the Toyman was sure to put a lot of colors, and pretty ones, too, on all the things he made for the Three Happy Children.

There is one good thing about all the animals in that Noah's Ark. They are very cunning and look like the real thing, but, as the Toyman said, "You can invite them to your house any time and they won't fight, or bite, or scratch, or quarrel. They are very polite and well-behaved."

Marmaduke had many a celebration for them, and

made many a glorious speech to them as well, and they listened to every word.

So the birthday party really lasted long after the seven candles had gone out, and the cake had gone, too, every crumb.

IX

DR. PHILEMON PIPP,
THE PATIENT MEDICINE MAN

Uncle Roger lived in town, quite a distance from the home of the Three Happy Children. When they walked, Marmaduke's short legs took one whole hour to reach it; Jehosophat's, forty-five minutes; though the Toyman's long shanks could cover the ground in fifteen. But then he could go ever so fast. However, they usually rode, and horses can always go faster than men. Even Old Methusaleh could trot there in twelve, and he was spavined and a little wind-broke, while Teddy and Hal, who were young and frisky, could get there as quick as a wink.

On this particular day Uncle Roger and Aunt Mehitable had a family party. It was a fine one, you may be sure, but we are not going to tell you about it, when something even more interesting happened that night.

At half-past eight the last horn sounded and the party was over. Mother and Hepzebiah climbed in the surrey, and, with them, two great-aunts, Sophronisba and Abigail. Aunt Phrony weighed more than three hundred pounds, but Aunt Abby only a hundred; and they were planning to visit the White House With the

Green Blinds by the Side of the Road - "for a week," they said, but the boys heard Father whisper to Mother, as he piled their baggage under the tailboard, - "From the size of those bags it looks like a year and a day." The boys wondered what that extra day could ever be for - probably to move all that baggage.

Now Teddy the Buckskin Horse was hitched to the surrey; and in the shafts of the buggy stood Hal the Red Roan. And that night the boys particularly wanted to ride behind Teddy. They liked to watch the black stripe that ran down his yellow back skim ahead of them over the road, just like a snake. And they liked the surrey, too. It had a fringe all around the top, and high mudguards, and a whip with a tassel and ribbon on it. But now that the great-aunts were in, Aunt Abby's side rose way up in the air, she was so light, but Aunt Phrony's sank down until the steel springs of the carriage groaned and scrunched on the axles. The surrey looked like a boat when all the passengers rush to one side to see who has fallen over.

There was no room for the boys, so they had to climb in the buggy. But, after all, the Toyman was to drive, and that quite made up for it. He might even let them drive, or tell them stories - about Ole Man Pumpkin, or the stars, or the cowboys out West, or any one of a number of wonderful things. So they were quite content as the Toyman said "Gee-dap," and they drove off through the night.

They had gone but a short distance when they saw a light. It was different from all the lights in the houses and the street lamps on the corners, which shone steadily and all the while. This one flickered and flared like a fire in the wind; and it smoked rather badly, too.

Jehosophat and Marmaduke tried to guess what it was, but neither was right. When they reached the corner of the street and got out of the buggy, they saw a lot of boys, big boys and little boys, and men, too, crowding around a wagon. The horses which had brought it there were tied to a hitching post a little way off, and a man stood in the back by the tailboard. The light which they had seen from afar shone over his head, a strange sort of torch, and was fed with oil by a little metal pan with a tube running to it. And it flickered oddly up and down, and from side to side, throwing funny shadows on the man, who looked queer enough himself.

He had long black hair like Buffalo Bill, and a long black coat - *very* long, with a fur collar on it.

Marmaduke whispered to the Toyman, -

"Can't you cure the man's coat? It's got the mange."

And the Toyman replied, -

"No, money is all that can cure that, and pretty soon he's going to get plenty from these people's pockets."

Marmaduke's eyes bulged.

"Is he a robber?" he asked in an awed whisper.

The Toyman laughed.

"Well, some folks might call him that without being sued for libel, but I 'spose he's within the law."

Marmaduke wondered how he could be in the law and in the wagon at the same time, and the Toyman had to explain that he meant that the strange man *ought* to go to jail, but probably wouldn't. Just why, he told them to "wait and see."

But, oh, we forgot - what was most important, - on the man's head was a tall silk hat. It looked as if it needed the mange cure quite as much as did the fur collar of his coat. And it was tipped on the side of his head, like a crazy old mill Marmaduke had seen once, that was about to fall in the river.

Behind the man was spread a banner with the man's name on it, Dr. Philemon Pipp, and a big chart like those the teachers used in school.

"Whew!" whistled Jehosophat, "look at that ole bag of bones!"

For on that chart was a big picture of a skeleton, and, by the side of the skeleton, other pictures, of a man with his skin taken off, which showed his bones, and his muscles, and all his insides - very prettily painted in blue and yellow and red.

That wasn't all there was on that wonderful wagon. Behind the chart, they saw lots of bottles filled with nice black juice. It looked like licorice water, and it made anyone's mouth water just to look at it!

But the man, Dr. Philemon Pipp, was talking.

And as he talked, he made queer gestures with his arms, as if he wanted to scoop up all the people - or something the people had - into his wagon. Perhaps it was their money he wanted to scoop up, though he said nothing - as to that, just, -

"Now, gents, step up a little closer, pleeze."

Then he tilted his hat on the other side of his head, and put one hand across his chest, the middle finger between the buttons of his vest, and all in a very grand way.

"Tonight," he went on, "for youah entertainment, I will oferrr this distinguished audience a marrvelous programme - an extrahorrrdinary exheebeeshun of tricks and sleight of hand meeraculs such as nevah befoh were puhfomed by human hands.

"Now watch, ladees, and keep yuh eyes peeled, gents - and mebbe youall kin learn the secret."

Then he had to stop for a minute, for the small boys were climbing on the hubs of the wheels.

"Heah, young man," he shouted, "have youall fohgot yuh mannahs? Do not futhuh disturb muh discourse."

Of course, Jehosophat and Marmaduke couldn't understand all these magnificent words, but they sounded quite splendid. No wonder the hat was so big, when it had to cover a head with such long words inside.

Now Dr. Philemon Pipp had turned to the crowd.

"Have any of you gents got a quatah? - Thank you, sah," he said to a man who handed him the money.

Then he took the silver quarter and asked a little boy to step up on the wagon. Jehosophat wished he had been asked, so that he could have learned the wonderful trick.

And now Dr. Pipp showed the coin to the little boy.

"You see it, young man?" he asked.

"Yes sir, yes sir," said the little boy, all excitement.

Ah, but the man was wiggling his hands through the air, saying, -

"Now you see it and now you don't."

And presto! he took that very same quarter which had been in his hand, out of - where do you think? - why, right out of the boy's mouth. That wasn't all, either, for next minute he took it out of his cap, then out of his ears. There had been one quarter before - now in his hand there were - five - shiny - quarters! It was a wonderful trick!

But now the strange man, Dr. Philemon Pipp, was speaking again.

"Now that you all understand the trick," he declared, "I will pefohm another foh youah entahtainment."

The funny thing about it was that no one understood it at all - except the Toyman.

"Do you really?" the boys asked him, and he replied, -

"Pshaw! that's easy, but watch, sonny, and see what he'll try next."

Meanwhile the man had taken off his tall silk hat.

"You see this hat, ladees an' gents? Just a simple piece

of headwear that has seen many suns and rains. No false bottom or top."

And he tapped the hat to show them it was just an ordinary hat. Still, Marmaduke thought it was very much out of the ordinary. Never had he seen such a grand one - not even on Deacon Smithers.

"Now peel yuh eyes - careful - watch - everybody ready? Presto, chango - and here we are."

And believe it or not as you may, out of that hat he drew a white rabbit - a real live white rabbit. He held it up by its ears for all to see.

And again he said, -

"Now that youall undahstand this simple little trick, I will -"

And again no one understood how to do it but the Toyman.

However, they just had to listen, for it was a wonderful speech.

"Ladees an' gents and fellow citizens of - " the strange man paused, coughed, then leaned down to his helper. "What's the name of this burg, Jake?" he whispered to him. "Ah, yes, fellow citizens of the glorious ceety of Five Corners -"

And Jehosophat whispered to the Toyman, -

"How does he know it's so glorious when he can't even remember the name?"

The Toyman chuckled and replied, -

"Oh, he's a remarkable man, the Doctor, a very remarkable man. But listen, boy, listen, you'll never hear the like again."

So of course they listened - with all their ears, and their eyes and their mouths, too.

"I will introjooce to you," went on the grand speech, "the famous Indian" - yes, that's just what he said, - "the famous Indian, Chief-Afraid-of-a-Rat. Come on, Chief, don't scare the ladies, and don't scalp the little boys as long as they're good."

Then up on that wagon stepped a big Indian with moccasins on his feet, and a dress of deerskin with beads embroidered on it, and a headdress of many feathers and many colors too. He opened his mouth wide, and said something that sounded like a speech and yet like a song: -

"Ging-goo, ging goo, ging goo!
Tunk a tin, tunk a tin, tunk a tin!
Geegry goo, geegry goo,
All-a-man lissen!"

That's what the Red Indian with all the feathers said, and it sounded very impressive.

As it was so hard for anyone who didn't know the real Indian language to understand, the man with the long hair and tall silk hat, this wise Dr. Philemon Pipp, explained it.

"The noble red man, the last of his tribe, Chief-Afraid-

Robert Gordon Anderson

of-a-Rat," said he, "is a great medicine man. He says that from his native soil he has distilled a wonderrful medicine that works like magic."

Then, wetting his lips, he leaned over and picked up one of the big bottles that was full of black juice like the water the children used to make from licorice sticks.

"If yuh have a pain or an ache, a misery in yuh back, if yuh suffah from stomach-ache or tooth-ache, or an ache in the head; if yuh feet burn and blister; if yuh tongue evah feels thick; if yuh feel a leetle inclined to dizzyness - in fact, if yuh have any ache or trouble in the world, this medicine will cure yuh, will bring instant relief."

Then he took another bottle and said some more:

"One bottle of this medicine is worth five dollahs. Who would not give a paltry five dollahs for to be cured of his miseries? But - ladees and gents, because I was once born in your beautiful ceety I will sell -"

"Why, he even forgot its name," whispered Jehosophat.

"Shush," whispered the Toyman right back at him, "don't give him away."

But, instead, of Jehosophat giving him away, it seemed Dr. Pipp was going to give something away himself, for he was saying in his speech, -

"Because I was once born in your beautiful ceety, I will give away - for this night only - a whole bottle of this magic medicine for the trifling sum of fifty cents!"

That was very generous, thought the boys, and they said so to the Toyman, but again he told them to "wait an' see."

And then Dr. Philemon Pipp turned to the crowd of men and boys and hollered real loud like the minister at camp-meeting, -

"Who'll be the first to be cuhed? Who'll be the first to be happy again?"

And one by one the silly people went down in their pockets, and brought up their fifty-cent pieces, and handed them up to the man on the wagon.

You see, every one must have had at least one of the kinds of pains and aches Dr. Pipp talked about, for he mentioned every one in the world.

Marmaduke thought that black medicine would be fine for the Toyman.

"Toyman," he said, "buy a bottle, an' it will cure you of that bad rheumatism."

"No," replied the Toyman, "that won't cure even chilblains. That old codger's not telling the truth. And the people are fools to believe him."

But all this time Dr. Pipp was handing out the bottles with one hand, and collecting the fifty-cent pieces with the other, and the Red Indian was singing his funny song, -

"Ging goo, ging goo,
Hunk-a-tin, hunk-a-tin, hunk-a-tin,

Geegry goo, geegry goo,
All-a-man lissen!"

And the light nickered on the funny pictures of the skeleton and the man with his skin off, and then on Dr. Philemon Pipp with his long black hair and tall silk hat, and on the feathers of the Red Indian, as he danced up and down singing that funny song.

At last something stranger still happened.

The Toyman had just muttered to himself, -

"They're fools, they are, but I guess I ought to stop him."

And just as he said this, Dr. Philemon saw him in the crowd. The Doctor must have felt hurt because the Toyman hadn't bought any of his bottles, for he pointed a finger with a great long nail right at the Toyman and said:

"Yuh sah, aren't yuh willin' to be cuhed?"

Now the Toyman was forever saying funny and surprising things, but he never said anything funnier and more surprising in his life than what he told that patent-medicine man.

"No, thank you, Mr. Steve Jorkins" - that's just what he called him, not Dr. Pipp at all - "that medicine of yours isn't magic. It wouldn't even cure a chicken of the pip."

Then all the men crowded around the Toyman, calling him by his old name.

"Do you know him, Frank? Is he fooling us?"

"You bet he is," replied the Toyman, "and he's got all your hard-earned money in his jeans."

Then he called to the boys to "come quick," for he thought there would be trouble, and there was.

For all those men and boys in the crowd climbed up on the wagon - and they grabbed Dr. Philemon Pipp by his fine fur collar - and they made him give back their money, every last cent of it. Then, while some of them held him, the others smashed all his bottles until the black juice ran over the tailboard like a dark waterfall, and they hurled his high silk hat on the top of the lamp-post, yelling, -

"You git out of here, quick! Come, skedaddle!"

And since, in his fright, he didn't "skedaddle" fast enough to suit them, they threw beets and all sorts of vegetables at him, vegetables that had been ripe a very long time. So at last the tall Doctor with his fine fur collar - but without his silk hat - hitched up his horses with trembling fingers, and he and his helper Jake and the Red Indian drove out of town "lickety-split." You could hear the wagon-wheels rattling away long after he turned the corner.

Then the Toyman "tlucked" to Hal and they drove off, too.

"How did you know him?" Jehosophat asked, after they had trotted a little way.

"Oh, I used to know him out West. He didn't remember me, but I did *him*. I bought one of his bottles once."

"Is he a robber?"

"Well, he calls himself a patent-medicine man, but I'd call him a 'fakir.'"

"What's a 'fakir,' Toyman?" put in Marmaduke, very sleepily.

"Oh, a man who pretends to be something he isn't, and who sells folks something that's no good, and takes all their money for nothing. But" - and he laughed - "some folks like to be fooled."

"It's too bad!" sighed Marmaduke.

"What's too bad, sonny?"

"Why, to smash all those big bottles and waste all that lovely licorice water."

But he soon forgot all about the bottles and the licorice water, and the bad Doctor Pipp with the tall hat and the fur collar, and the Red Indian, too, for, as they rode along by the River, the Moon was up, and seemed to be riding along with them - never getting ahead or behind, just keeping even with Hal the Red Roan. And Marmaduke loved to go riding or walking with a great yellow moon. Besides, the Toyman told them a story, as he had promised - and a nice one it was - so the little boy fell asleep.

But I wouldn't say that they never dreamed about that fur collar, and the tall hat, and the Indian, and all those bottles.

It's just possible that they did.

Robert Gordon Anderson

X

WHEN JEHOSOPHAT FORGOT HIS PIECE

There was much excitement in the Red Schoolhouse. Examinations were over; books laid aside. And the walls re-echoed to thrilling sounds, - to happy voices and shuffling feet, to poetry, marches, and songs. They were practising for Commencement, for Closing Day. And at home the parents were busy, too, making white dresses and sashes for the girls, buying new suits for the boys in town, or making some over from father's old trousers.

Marmaduke was to take part in the marches and songs, but Jehosophat had to speak a whole piece, all alone too. It was a great honor, no doubt about that, which Jehosophat didn't appreciate. He thought it a bother.

Now their teacher was a patriot and fond of History. All through the term she had told them tales of brave lads who were good and great. Probably she wanted them to become good and great, too, and of course it was the thing to be. That Jehosophat knew, but it was pretty hard when one kept forgetting.

So he wasn't at all sure of himself, but of one thing he *was* sure, - the stories were lost on Fatty. Try as he would he never could think of *him* as being "good and great," or exactly "a hero."

But that was the least of Jehosophat's worries. He had been given a piece to learn - to recite before a big crowd!

It was poetry - all about a boy who had stuck by his ship and gone down with it, too. The piece was called by the boy's name - a queer sort of word - Casabianca. If the piece was as hard as its name, Jehosophat thought he never would learn it.

"Well, Jehosophat," said his father that night, "how's the orator?"

But Mother said, -

"Don't tease him, Will, I'm sure he'll do us proud."

Jehosophat squirmed in his seat. He didn't want to "do anyone proud." That was not his ambition. And he squirmed still more when she asked him, -

"Have you learned it all, Jehosophat?"

He mumbled something that sounded like, -

"Donev'nknownameyet."

So next day when he came back from school he had to stay in the parlour to study it.

After a while - not so long a while, either - he called to Mother, -

"Mother, I think I could learn it a lot better out doors

Robert Gordon Anderson

than in this dark room."

"All right, dear," she said, "if you're sure you won't let anything distract you."

"No, Mother, I promise." And he went out by the big elm and stood under the Oriole's nest. "The boy stood on the burning deck Whence all but he had fled."

That is the way it began and he started:

"The boy stood on the burning deck" - then he had to stop, for Mr. Stuck-up, the Turkey, was taking his afternoon parade right near him. Mr. Stuckup didn't seem to like that piece at all. Neither did Jehosophat, for that matter.

"'The boy'" - he began again.

"Gobble, gobble," shrieked the Turkey.

"'Stood on the burning -'"

"Gobble, gobble," again rudely interrupted Mr. Stuckup.

So Jehosophat went around to the side of the house by the Lilac Bush. He stood up straight and tried it all over again.

"'The boy stood on the burning deck' - *get down, get down*!" he yelled. Now that was strange. It sounded as if he were telling the boy to get down off that deck. But it was only Wienerwurst he was talking to. For, when he made that fine gesture which Teacher had shown them, Wienerwurst, who had crept up behind him, thought his master was playing some game, and jumped up at his outstretched fingers.

So once more Jehosophat picked up his reader, and walked over to the Crying Tree, whose green willow branches trailed in the Pond.

He practised his fine bow for a while, then began. This time he actually got through the first verse all right, and was quite pleased with himself. But no sooner had he stopped than he heard behind him -

A loud

"HISS! HISS!"

Now it isn't pleasant to try to make a good speech, and have some one hiss you when they ought to be clapping their hands. But that is just what The Foolish White Geese were doing to Jehosophat.

Once more he picked up his reader, and marched way up the Brook. He had just begun the lines all over again when Miss Cross Patch the Guinea Hen ran out from behind the barn and screeched horribly - just as he was making that fine gesture, too.

"GAWKE'E! - GAWKE'E! - GAWKE'E!"

Now to be called gawky when he thought the gesture was particularly graceful, was indeed discouraging. And, to add to his discomfort, when he tried it again - for the hundredth time, it seemed - the cows in the pasture stretched their red muzzles over the bars and called:

"BOOOOOOO!"

- just as if they wanted him to stop. And the horses whinnied:

"FUNN-NN-NN-NNY!"

It was no use, so Jehosophat rushed into the house again, stuffed some cotton in his ears, and went up in the attic, where he was sure he wouldn't be disturbed.

Here he succeeded pretty well, and had learned two verses, and the name - which was quite important - when the supper bell rang. So he felt he had earned that nice glass of creamy milk, and the big slice of gingerbread, especially the thick chocolate icing on top. It was an extra thick piece, too, which Mother gave him, probably as a prize for all his hard work.

Next morning, on the way to school, he was reciting Casabianca for practice. He tried it on the Purple Crackles that flew in the fields by the blackberry bushes; the little Gold Finches that swayed on the grasses; and the topknotted Kingbirds on the telegraph wires overhead.

And he thought he was getting on pretty well with "The boy stood on the burning deck," when a voice took the second line right out of his mouth:

"Eating peanuts by the peck!!!!!"

Angrily he turned, and there were Fatty Hamm and Reddy Toms, Dicky Means too, and Lizzie Fizzletree, all making faces at him and mocking him with funny gestures. Surely no teacher ever taught gestures like those.

They began it all over again, reciting together. And this is the piece they made of it - you never would have recognized poor Casabianca at all:

"The boy stood on the burning deck
Eating peanuts by the peck.
His father called, he would not go
Because he loved his peanuts so!!!"

"Stop," yelled Jehosophat, "that isn't it at all."

"'Tis, too," shouted Fatty and the others together, and they repeated in one breath, as fast as they could:

"'Sfathercalled andewouldn'tgo
Causeeloved 'ispeanutsso."

Yes, every time Jehosophat tried to tell them what it *really* was, they kept shouting in singsong voices, faster and faster:

"Fathercalled 'ewoodengo
Causeeloved 'ispeanutsso."

And every once in a while that little imp Lizzie Fizzletree would make outrageous bows, almost down to the ground, in imitation of Jehosophat.

Next day was *the* day, the *great* day. And all the boys came dressed in new suits, or suits made over from Father's old trousers, with stiff collars, and ties of red, or blue, or brown; and the girls had pretty white dresses with sashes sticking out like butterflies' wings.

Jehosophat thought they did resemble butterflies until he looked down at their feet; and then very crossly he decided that those feet spoiled "the *effect*." You see, he was getting to use and to think in big words now.

But while he was looking at the regiment of feet, along came Mr. Humbleby, the Presidentboardofeducation, and all the County Trustees, and the proud parents from near and from far. You could see a long line of buggies and surries and carryalls lined against the fence.

Then the signal was given, and the Teacher took her pointer and rose, and the scholars smoothed their sashes, or their hair, and rose, too; and one and all sang, -

"My country, 'tis of thee."

Then there were more songs by Theentireschool and pieces by the scholars. Lizzie Fizzletree tried one all about flowers. "The Fringed Gentian," it was called, and it was very pretty. But when Lizzie got through with it, Jehosophat didn't think it was so beautiful. She recited it something like this:

"Dear flo'wr so cal'm and pu're and bri'ght That op'nest in' the qu'i-et nig'ht."

And as she recited it she made gestures in all directions, first to one side, then to the other, just such floppy gestures as Ole Man Scarecrow would have made. That is, sometimes they looked like that, and sometimes her arms looked like the arms of a windmill. And her frizzy pigtails swished around with her arms - just like the sails of a windmill that had suddenly gone mad. The people started to titter, and Jehosophat started to giggle with them, when suddenly he thought of his own plight, and little shivers ran up and down his back, and his face felt very flushed and warm.

Then there were more songs by "Theentireschool" - and more pieces. My, would they never end! And then there were speeches by the Presidentboardeducation and the Trustees, who seemed to appreciate the privilege more than most of the pupils, Jehosophat thought, for they never stopped when they had the chance.

He looked out of the window. Over by the orchard, he could hear a flicker go "Rat-a-tat-tat," boring away at the old apple tree. The sun was shining nice and warm, and he wondered if he couldn't climb up on his seat, and drop out of the open window, and run away ever so far. He was supposed to "do his parents proud"; and if there was anything he hated, it was "doing somebody proud." Oh, golly!

"The boy stood on the burning deck."

Once or twice he repeated it to himself. Yes, he knew it all right. But just then Fatty Hamm, who sat behind him, leaned over and whispered, -

"Don't forget the peanuts, Joshy!"

Jehosophat frowned and tried not to pay any attention, but the Presidentboardeducation had taken out his spectacles and was reading from a paper.

"Recitation by -." He couldn't seem to understand the

name and put on his glasses a little nearer the end of his nose,

"Recitation by *Je-hos-o-phat Green*!"

How loud it sounded!

The Presidentboardeducation was looking all over the room.

"Come, come," he said, "*where* is Jehosophat?"

Now that boy couldn't rise, for the tail of his jacket had slid down in the crack of the seat, and Fatty Hamm was holding it tight so he couldn't even move.

Again the spectacles of the Presidentboardeducation looked over the children in grave surprise. They lighted on Jehosophat.

"Come, come, my little man, there's nothing to be afraid of."

And the Presidentboardeducation smiled on him, with that sort of smile "grownups" always put on when they're going to "do something for your good," like pulling a tooth, for instance, or offering you castor oil.

There was a drone, too, of voices like the bees outside, and all eyes were looking at him. He didn't dare look at his mother, who was hoping so hard that he would "do her proud," or at his father, either. But he did glance once at the Toyman, who was sitting, looking very uncomfortable, in a boiled shirt and a stiff collar that almost choked his adam's apple. His hair was slicked down extra tight, too, and he kept gazing down into his new store hat. He felt very sorry for himself, and even sorrier for Jehosophat.

But the Presidentboardeducation was saying, -

"Come, come," again, and then, -

"Tut, tut!"

And all-of-a-sudden Fatty let go of his coat, and Jehosophat found himself on his feet and on his way to the platform.

He wanted to take a little of the glass of water that stood by the Presidentboardeducation - just one little sip - for his throat felt so dry and his tongue stuck to the roof of his mouth. But he couldn't.

He made the fine bow all right, and Mother looked at Father as much as to say, -

"There, I knew our boy could do it."

And wonderfully he got through the first line, - "The boy stood on the burning deck."

But then he just had to look at Fatty, and Fatty had just put a peanut up to his mouth - as a sort of signal, I guess.

"The boy stood on the burning deck," repeated Jehosophat, forgetting the next line, and so having to stick to the first. He couldn't think of anything but Fatty's grinning mouth and that peanut.

"The boy stood on the burning deck," he called, louder

than before.

"The boy stood on the burning deck," still louder.

"Yes, yes, my little man," said the Presidentboard-education, still with that smile that Jehosophat hated so, and before he knew it he was shouting right back at the spectacles: -

"Eating peanuts by the peck.
His father called 'e wouldngo
Causehelovedispeanutsso!"

Yes sir, he shouted the last line oh, so loud, like a little bull, right in the Presidentboardeducation's face. And the Presidentboardeducation was so startled that he almost knocked the pitcher of water off the table. And the teacher's glasses fell off her nose, and she seemed to be unable to find them in her embarrassment - and then - the whole audience roared till the walls of the little Red Schoolhouse echoed to their laughter, and Jehosophat saw Fatty slapping his fat legs in delight.

Meanwhile, Jehosophat wasn't losing any time. He just hurried to the window, climbed up on the seat, then on the sill, and dropped on the soft grass below, and ran up the road towards home, just as fast as he could travel.

He hadn't gone far when he heard someone calling, -

"Hey, Sonny!"

He turned with relief.

There was the Toyman, his long legs fast catching up

with the runaway. And the same old smile was on the Toyman's face.

And when the long legs had caught up with the short ones, the Toyman put his arm around the boy's shoulders, and they walked along like - well, like two old chums.

What was finest, too, was that he never mentioned the cause of Jehosophat's trouble and embarrassment, which is what no really true friend ever should do.

At last Jehosophat asked, -

"Where we goin'?"

"Let's go fishin' - I hate speeches," the Toyman replied.

"I made a silly, a fool of myself, didn't I?" said Jehosophat.

"Not by a long sight," the Toyman replied. "You see, sonny," he went on to explain, very soberly, "that's an old piece of yours and out of date. Now they're making new arrangements and editions of books and po'try all the time. They just change with the times. And yours is a heap better than the old piece, anyway you look at it."

Jehosophat wasn't quite so sure. But, anyway, they had a great time "fishin'."

Robert Gordon Anderson

XI

OLE MAN PUMPKIN

It was October, and the cornfield was deserted and bare. Jehosophat and Marmaduke could remember it as a more beautiful picture. For there, in the Summer, an army had camped, the great army of the corn, with tassels and tall yellow spears, and bright green banners waving and tossing in the wind. But when Fall had come, Father and the Toyman had come, too, with their sickles like swords, to attack and cut down that brave army. And now the corn soldiers were all laid away, stiff and cold, in the barn, or else in the silo - to be pickled in juice!

Marmaduke and Jehosophat looked over the field. It was covered with little hills, and there the feet of the corn soldiers still stood, all that was left of them, for they had been "swished by those swords," just at the ankles.

Between the hills shone the last of the pumpkins, big, round and yellow - red-yellow like an orange. Most of them had gone in the wagon, long ago, but the largest of all had been left. My, but he was a big fellow! "The biggest in the world!" they declared.

He had been saved for the great day - or night, we

should say - Hallowe'en.

But let's hurry the clock - over three days - to the morning before the celebration.

The three children were watching Mother in the kitchen. She was busy with the big pumpkin, but the Toyman had to help her with it - it was so huge. He lifted it on the table - then - what do you think?

He took a sharp knife and scalped that Pumpkin - just like an Indian - cut a great hole in his head. Then Mother scooped out his insides and chopped them up fine. Ole Man Pumpkin was very brave, just stood it and said never a word.

"Why, he doesn't holler a bit!" exclaimed Marmaduke. "*I* would, if anybody scalped *me* and took *my* insides out!"

Next, Mother brought out the big pot, filling it part with water, and part with Ole Man Pumpkin's yellow insides. And the fire roared angrily and boiled them, boiled them all up. It took quite a long time, but the children didn't grow tired - it was such a mysterious, such an interesting process.

At last Mother decided it had been cooked long enough, and she poured the water into the sink, the nice yellow stuff into a bowl. Then she mashed the lumps till it looked like golden mush.

Now the flour was sifted on the pastry board, and the dough rolled until it was as smooth and flat as a sheet or counterpane. Then quickly and neatly the dough counterpanes were placed in the pans, hanging over the edges like covers overlapping a bed. Taking a knife, Mother cut off these edges even with the pan, then, for decoration, made little marks in the dough all around, like the flutings of the Fairy Lamp.

Of course, the insides of Ole Man Pumpkin wouldn't taste quite right as they were, so Mother broke some eggs over them, adding some milk and a pinch of spice for seasoning, and the delicious mess was stirred till all was thoroughly mixed.

Soon it was ready, a fine filling for pies and pans or little boys or kings, for that matter, and she scraped it into the pans until the white crust was covered up, all but the fluted edges. Then into the oven went the pies, on the top shelf, and the door was closed to keep the heat in.

Meanwhile the children had been so busy watching Mother and those pies; and their mouths had watered so as they watched, that they hadn't noticed the Toyman at all - until they heard him say, -

"Good mornin', Jack!"

Jack Who? Not Jack Holmes or Jack Frost - no, it was someone much handsomer, although he had a hole in the top of his head, a fat face, big round eyes, a large flat nose, and a wide, wide mouth with lots of square teeth in it.

"Mr. Jehosophat Green," said the Toyman very politely, "let me make you acquainted with Jack, or, as he is sometimes called, 'Ole Man Pumpkin.'"

Jehosophat bowed low.

"Pleased to meet you," he said, just like grownup folks.

Then Marmaduke piped up, -

"Make me acquainted, too."

"To be sure," said the Toyman, "Mr. Marmaduke Green meet Mr. Jack Lantern."

"*Very* glad to know you," said Marmaduke, bowing even lower than had Jehosophat, while Hepzebiah, dancing in her eagerness, shouted, -

"Make me 'quainted, make me 'quainted!"

The Toyman took her by the arm, and he in turn made a grand bow.

"Now, Jack, old fellow, this is an honor. Here's a lady expressin' a desire to make your acquaintance. Miss Hepzebiah Green, let me present Mr. Jack O. Lantern, otherwise known as 'Ole Man Pumpkin.'"

Then he turned to Jack.

"You don't mind my calling you so familiarly, do you?"

Apparently Jack didn't mind, for he just squatted there, lazy-like, and grinned with all his big square teeth.

Hepzebiah giggled back at him. She was having a glorious time. So were they all.

So, through that long - no, very *short* - afternoon, the kitchen was filled with pleasant smells and the air of fun and a pleasant surprise to come. They almost thought they could *smell* the surprise as well as the pies.

It came at last, that is the surprise did, for, just after supper, the Toyman disappeared, probably to do some of his chores.

A little while later there came a tap at the window.

Marmaduke turned.

Jehosophat turned.

Hepzebiah turned.

"Ooh, ooh!" said she;

"Golly!" said Marmaduke; and

"Gee whiz!", Jehosophat.

Great yellow eyes looked in through the window, and a nose, and a great grinning mouth with big teeth in it.

The visitor nodded, needing no introduction, for they had made his acquaintance already.

He came into the house, helped a little by the Toyman, and still nodding his great yellow head.

They gave him a seat of honor, not *by* the table, but *on* it, right in the centre. Marmaduke climbed up and looked down into the big hole in the top of his head. In it was a thick candle, dancing inside his old yellow skull, and he seemed a good comrade, that Ole

Man Pumpkin.

But what was the Toyman doing now?

He had a tub in his arms. He set it down, filled it with water, then popped three red apples in it.

And the children got down on their knees around the tub and tried to take the apples in their teeth. But round and round they bobbed, so fast that it was difficult to catch them.

"Ugh!" exclaimed Jehosophat;

"Kerchoo!" sneezed Marmaduke;

"Guhuh!" coughed Hepzebiah, all their eyes and their mouths, noses and tummies, too, full of water. And always those little red apples bobbed out of reach. Once Jehosophat thought he had caught one, but his teeth slipped on its smooth round cheek and all he got was a piece of skin. It was fun just the same.

A lot of other games they played, with flour, and candles, and rings, and things, then the Toyman gathered them up on his knees and the arm of his chair, and told them a story. A good one? Of course! He *never* told a poor one.

By this time the children were sneezing and Mother said they'd have to go to bed or they'd catch their "deathocold."

When they were at last undressed Jehosophat lay his head on the pillow. But it wouldn't stay down. He could see Ole Man Pumpkin sitting there on the dining-room table - so still! The Toyman had forgotten to put out the candle in his head. It was a thick candle, and it burned a long, long time. Ole Man Pumpkin seemed to be very cheerful with it inside his hollow skull. It made him feel "all lit up," he heard the Toyman say.

The big, round eyes never blinked. They just watched the little boy all the time, and the big mouth was "just laughin' an' laughin' an' laughin' at him."

Then all of a sudden Ole Man Pumpkin started to move. He didn't have any legs, but he slid from the table to the floor, and somehow climbed up on the window sill, and rolled out of the window. Jehosophat had to get out of bed to see what his new friend was going to do. He followed him across the dining room, over the window sill, and by the barn. And all the little boy had on were his pajamas, but he didn't feel cold, for Ole Man Pumpkin looked so bright and jolly and warm that Jehosophat felt bright and jolly and warm, too.

Ole Man Pumpkin kept bumping his way along to the cornfield where Mr. Scarecrow stood on guard, though his work for the year was done.

Now Mr. Scarecrow seemed to have a lot of friends around him, and he was making a speech. There was Ole Man Pumpkin, of course; and Jehosophat, who had just arrived; and Mr. Stuckup the Turkey, as usual looking very grand and proud; and the Hippity-hop Bunnies, wiggling their noses in their funny way; and Johnny Cottontail, their little wild cousin, making his nose go, too. And there was Reddy Fox, with one forepaw raised and his eyes as bright as beads; and a whole squad of corn-soldiers with yellow tassels and green banners and tall spears. My! but they looked bright and gay once more! And there were lots of funny little folk besides, - three bright rosy-cheeked Apples, talking and laughing and chattering away just like real people, and two Pie-pans, only they didn't look flat and dull as when they were in the kitchen, but had shiny intelligent faces, and they were chattering away, too.

Mr. Scarecrow was making a speech to them in such a ridiculous fashion. His arms stood out stiff and straight from the shoulder, but he made queer floppy gestures with his wrists.

"I'm a Red," he was saying, "and I call upon you to rise upon the cap'talists, who feed on your flesh and bones."

Jehosophat shuddered, for he thought he knew what was in Mr. Scarecrow's mind. That very day in school they had had "Currantyvents," and Miss Prue Parsons had told them a lot about Reds, and Annarkisseds, and Revolushions they wanted to start all over the world. Horrible, shivery things they were that she had told them!

"Revolt - rebel. Rebel - revolt!" Old Mr. Scarecrow shouted, flapping his wrists and swinging in the wind.

"Hear, hear!" cried the Little Red Apples;

"Hear, hear!" cried the Shiny Pie Pans; and

"Horrible, horrible!", Mr. Stuckup the Turkey.

Ole Man Pumpkin didn't say anything, but just grinned and grinned with his big eyes and old yellow teeth.

"There is a cap'talist now, standing before you!" shouted Mr. Scarecrow, and his wrists flapped right at Jehosophat, "away with him!"

"Away with him!" shouted one and all - the Little Red Apples, the Shiny Pie Pans, Mr. Stuckup the Turkey, and the Tall Corn Soldiers; and all the time Ole Man Pumpkin kept grinning and grinning, as if he were enjoying himself most cruelly.

Then Mr. Scarecrow said in a solemn voice:

"Soldiers, do your duty with the prisoner!"

And all at once two Tall Corn Soldiers stood on each side of him, grabbed him by one arm, and growled:

"About face - forward march!"

And the first thing he knew, he was being hustled very swiftly over towards the Pond.

The Little Red Apples and the Shiny Pie Pans rolled on ahead, chattering gaily to each other; Mr. Stuckup marched on very pompously; Ole Man Pumpkin bumped along just in front; the two Corn Soldiers marched by his side; and a lot of others pricked him from behind with their sharp, cruel spears.

What were they going to do with him? *That* was the question.

He was soon to know, for they had reached the edge of

the Pond.

"Duck him!" shouted the Little Red Apples in glee.

And the Tall Corn Soldiers seized Jehosophat by the hair on the top of his head, and shoved him under the water, way under, oh, way, way under.

"Give me a bite!" said the first Little Red Apple, snapping at their prisoner's face when he came to the surface again.

"Me, too!" shouted the second.

"A big one for me!" yelled the third, and they all rolled in the water and bobbed around, bumping up against his face and trying their best to take a nip out of his cheeks.

He never had known before that apples had teeth, but, sure enough, he felt them now - there was actually a little piece gone from each side of his face.

"Great fun, Hallowe'en!" they called to one another as they bobbed about, still snapping at his cheeks.

"Enough!" It was the two Corn Soldiers who spoke, and Jehosophat was dragged from the Pond. He was dripping wet and he felt pretty cold in his pajamas.

"Now it's my turn," said Ole Man Pumpkin. "Take him to the workshop, there's a lot of sharp tools there."

Tools! Whatever could they be going to do with him now! But he had no time to think, for there they were, all bumping, or rolling, or stalking along, to the workshop, and taking him with them. They had no keys, but they managed to enter just the same.

"On the table - come, up with him!"

And immediately the two Corn Soldiers siezed him by the arms and hoisted him on the table, where he sat in his little pajamas, like a tailor, with his knees crossed under him. But what was the idea? What was that Ole Man Pumpkin telling the Corn Soldiers?

"Just cut a little hole in the top of his head - just enough to scoop out his insides. Quick work, or he'll spoil."

"Save the drumstick for me," gobbled Mr. Stuck-up, "they didn't bother me much on Hallowe'en, but I'm going to get even for Thanksgiving."

And all the time the Little Red Apples rolled around the floor in high glee; and the Shiny Pie Pans danced against each other, making a noise like the cymbals of the Salvation Army parade; and Ole Man Pumpkin kept sharpening and sharpening his knife.

Then - then - but it was a new voice that was speaking to him.

"Get up!" it said.

It wasn't Ole Man Pumpkin that was telling him to get up on that table, so he could scalp him. It was Mother telling him to sit up in bed!

"I knew they had too much pie," she was saying, and, "come, dear, open your mouth; take this and you'll feel better in the morning."

She was on one side of the bed, and Father was on the other, ready to take a hand, as he always did under the circumstances.

They weren't pleasant, either, the circumstances, for they were, - first Father's grip on his arm, then a tablespoon - not a teaspoon, or a dessert spoon, but a tablespoon, such as a giant might use - full of a thick yellow liquid from that bottle they hated so, and pointed right at his tongue.

However, he took it pretty bravely, swallowed it, gulped, then choked back the tears. But the orange-juice, which followed the yellow stuff, almost made up for it. He always did like orange as a color better than yellow, any day.

And *there* was Ole Man Pumpkin again, on the dining room table, grinning, not wickedly but cheerfully. He winked at Jehosophat, just like the Ole Man in the Moon, whom he strangely resembled - as much as to say:

"We'll have a good time yet in spite of that bottle."

After all, he wasn't an enemy of the children, who would cut holes in their heads and scoop out their insides - he was their *friend*, was Ole Man Pumpkin, and Jehosophat felt much relieved at that.

XII

THE NORWAY SPRUCE

The Three Happy Children were looking at the calendar. It was a large one which had been given to Father by Silas Drown who kept the Hardware Store. On it was a picture of a meadow, with a green brook running through it; and people were haying in the meadow. It was undoubtedly a beautiful picture, but the children weren't interested in it at all. They were gazing at the numbers underneath.

Now one would suppose that nothing could be quite so dull as figures, or so uninteresting. But these told a very fascinating story. There were thirty-one of them, all in little black squares like those that make up a checkerboard. Thirty of the numbers were black like the squares, but one was red, bright red. And there lies the story. You see, there was a good reason for that one being red, oh, a very good reason!

Jehosophat took out a pencil and climbed on a chair, while Marmaduke and Hepzebiah looked on in wonder. The pencil made a mark at 23.

"Only two more days," said the older boy.

"Hooray!" exclaimed his brother.

"Hooway!" echoed their little sister.

Then they all sighed - three long-drawn out sighs - it was so hard to wait. And when they were through sighing, they all stood and stared at all those numbers, and particularly that bright 25, their eyes growing rounder each minute.

There was something in the air, most decidedly, something that the children couldn't exactly feel or touch or handle. It was as though the sky, and air, and the trees, and the house itself, were carrying a secret, a happy secret, and one almost too big to be kept.

They could get hints of that secret everywhere. Sometimes they caught Mother and Father whispering about things - very mysterious things. Mother, too, was working late these nights. What she was making they could never find out, though they looked and guessed and wondered.

The Toyman wouldn't let them in his shop. And Father, when he went to town, for once refused to let the children go with him and old Methusaleh.

But the closets were the most mysterious of all. Some of them were actually locked, and, though Marmaduke tried to peek through the keyholes, all he could see was darkness - like midnight.

Once Mother saw him peeking.

She went over to the door and unlocked it. But she didn't open it.

"I thought I would keep it locked, children," she said,

"but after all I've decided I won't. Trust is stronger than any key. And I think I can trust you, can't I?"

"Y-y-yes," said Jehosophat.

"Y-y-yes," said Marmaduke.

"Y-y-yeth," lisped Hepzebiah.

"Thank you, my dears," she said, then went away, leaving the door unlocked.

For two whole weeks they hadn't peeked. They had hung around that closet and stared and sighed, but never once did they even try the door. And I think they were rather brave, when they knew there were packages inside, all wrapped in red paper and tied with green ribbon, and they could almost hear the paper rustle. Oh, well they knew those packages were there, for hadn't they caught Mother inside with her apron over packages and things, the bits of red and green showing through the folds of the apron. Besides that, they had seen Father go to the largest closet of all with parcels covered by a blanket. And it is very hard to know that there are things, wonderfully beautiful things like treasures, hidden in dark closets, and not to be able to investigate and find out about them. But then, of course, there was the fun of guessing. And they guessed everything under the sun, enough toys and articles to fill the biggest store in the world, or the whole of Santa Claus' workshop, which stands under the North Star where the polar bears live and the Aurora weaves pretty scarfs in the sky.

Well, that day passed, and in the morning Jehosophat climbed on a chair again and put a little mark through the next number - 24.

"Tomorrow!" he said in a solemn whisper. And the whispers of the other two children, echoing him, were quite as full of wonder and awe.

Then they went to the window. Snow was on the ground.

"It's as white as the feathers of the Foolish White Geese," Jehosophat happened to remark.

"No, it's prettier than that," Marmaduke corrected him. "It's like the coats of the Hippity-Hop Bunnies. And the sky is just as gray as the Quaker ladies over in the meeting-house on Wally's creek," he added.

That afternoon they heard sleigh-bells, clear, tinkling, but never jangling, on the still air.

"Whoa!" yelled the Toyman.

The big sleigh stopped by the side porch. Hal the Red Roan and Teddy the Buckskin Horse tossed their heads merrily, and the sleigh-bells jingled even after the team had come to a halt.

"All aboard!" shouted the Toyman, as he stamped the snow from his boots and entered the kitchen. "We're going to find the biggest, finest tree in the whole woods! Who wants to go?"

Who wouldn't want to go! There was a scurrying for boots and coats, mufflers and mittens. Then they tumbled in, the sleighbells jingled, and off they flew through the deep, powdery, sparkling snow.

The river was not in motion; it was not flowing at all this day, but lay like a long lead pipe, twisting between the white snow banks. Sometimes, when the sun came out and shone upon it, the lead was changed to pearl.

They drove away from it now, up by Jake Miller's place, and past the Fizzletrees' and the Van Nostrands', then up the hill to the woods.

The trees stood still like a great congregation, Marmaduke thought. There were giant oaks, their heavy branches all gnarled and twisted; tall chestnuts with rough gray trunks; shaggy hickories with bark always ready to peel off like "proud flesh"; little ironwood trees whose wood was so tough that the axe must be sharp to cut them at all; and silver birches, gracefully swaying in the wind, and white against the snow. Most of them were naked and bare, but on the oaks and birches rustled a few little left-over leaves, brown and dried-up, and crackling and cackling like little old people. Ah! but everywhere, in, and around, and between, the naked trees, and on higher up the hill, were others still clothed in green, - trees that never cast off their cloaks, even when winter came, - spruces, cedars, firs, and hemlocks and pines. They were decorated, too, for on their green branches hung tufts of snow like the pieces of fur on the carriage robe of the neighbor's baby.

The Toyman tied the horses to the fence-rail and they all jumped out of the sleigh. He lifted little Hepzebiah, then started to help Marmaduke.

"No, thank you," said that little boy, "I don't need any help," and, all alone, he climbed over the fence after his big brother.

Then on they tramped, through the snow, and under the branches and around the bushes, looking for that great tree which soon was to have the place of honor in their house.

"There's one," said Marmaduke.

"No," replied the Toyman, "that won't do. See-it has clumps of needles like a porcupine's quills. It looks beautiful in the woods, but it wouldn't look so pretty in the parlor. And that cedar yonder is too thick to hang the presents and the ornaments on. - Yes, that hemlock is pretty, and that fir - but I guess we'll stick to the spruce. Let's find one that's shapely and just the right height."

So they hunted around until he said:

"Now there's a likely young spruce."

It was covered with little needles that ran evenly all along the twigs, leaving plenty of room on the branches for all they were going to put on them. And it looked very soft and feathery and green against the snow.

The Toyman looked up at the topmost twig, carefully measuring it with his eye.

"It will just about reach the parlor ceiling," he declared, and the boys guessed so, too.

Then he took the axe from his shoulder.

"Stand back, fellows," he shouted, "and watch the chips fly!"

Crack! went the sharp axe blade. A little cut appeared in the tree, about fifteen inches above the ground. Crack! again, and a little cut appeared in the trunk, about four inches under the other mark. Crack! again, and a piece of wood flew out of the spruce.

"A little farther back, youngsters!" called the Toyman, and the children sought the shelter of the big oak nearby.

Fast flew the axe, still faster the white chips. My! how strong the Toyman was! Now a big hole yawned in the trunk of the spruce, like the jaws of the alligator when he basks in the sun. It grew wider and wider. The Toyman looked around to make sure that the children were well out of harm's way, then he swung once more, one great hefty stroke, and with a great crash the spruce fell and measured its length in the snow. And the Toyman put the axe and the tree too, over his shoulder - he certainly was strong, that Toyman - and through the woods they tramped back again, and loaded the tree on the sleigh.

Then he paused for a moment.

"Think a little jag of green would go nice on the windows," he remarked, "and a touch of red to brighten things up a bit."

So they looked and found plenty of green for wreaths, and some bayberries like coral, and some holly, besides, by the ruins of the deserted house that had burned down years before they were born.

It had been a long hunt and, though the sky had cleared, it was growing pretty dark when they climbed in the sleigh. As the Toyman clambered upon the seat and took the reins, he turned around and looked up the hill.

"The stars are beginning to twinkle," he said, "and look, youngsters, there is a whole army of Christmas trees for you."

They turned around and gazed in the direction in which his finger pointed, and there, sure enough, the evergreens, - the spruces, pines, and hemlocks, the firs, and the cedars, too, were standing so still, and the stars were peeping out between their twigs and branches all over the hill, twinkling like little candles. There were hundreds and hundreds of Christmas trees, standing up straight on that hill, with millions and millions of candles on them.

"My, but that's pretty!" the Toyman exclaimed.

As for the children, they said, "Oh," and "Ah," all in one breath. It was so wonderful to see all those live Christmas trees growing and shining in the forest.

"You see," the Toyman went on to explain, "that's how they first got the notion of a Christmas tree, seein' the little stars shine through the forest. - A good notion, too, I should say."

A good one? Why, the best in the world! So the Three Happy Children thought as they drove down the hill and back by the river.

And when they turned in the drive and Teddy and Hal walked off to the barn, the sleighbells jingling like Christmas chimes in the air, they shouted "hooray"

Robert Gordon Anderson

again, one and all.

Then Jehosophat said as they reached the door, -

"And now for tomorrow!" -

XIII

WHEN THE DOOR OPENED

And of course Tomorrow came, as it always does - only to become Today.

Jehosophat didn't climb on the chair that morning. There was no need of making black marks with his pencil, when that red number, 25, stood out above all the others, so bright in its scarlet splendor.

As a matter of fact, the children never looked at the calendar at all. They were too busy with their stockings. Now, ordinarily; stockings either hang limp on the line or else fit very evenly on smooth little legs. But the three which hung by the fireplace were stiff and queerly shaped, each full of knobs and bumps.

The children rose very early in the morning to get them, and were taking out the oranges, and apples, and tops, and nuts, and raisins, and marbles, and hair-ribbon (for Hepzebiah, of course) and the mouth-organs, tin wagons and candy-canes, when a voice called, "Merry Christmas," and Mother's face beamed in the doorway - then Father's. Soon there was a stamping of feet on the kitchen porch, and the Toyman came in from his milking and called, "Merry Christmas," too. And he and Mother and Father seemed to get more fun out of those stockings than the children themselves, or as much, which is saying a very great deal.

It was hard to dress properly that morning - and particularly hard to wash behind one's ears. Jehosophat put on one stocking inside out; Marmaduke his union suit outside in; and one of his shoes was button and the other lace. But they were all covered up, anyway, and Ole Northwind couldn't nip their flesh, and the Constable couldn't arrest them, so it was sufficient, I suppose.

How they did it, I don't know, but they managed to get through breakfast somehow. Then there was a glorious spinning of tops, and playing of mouth-organs, and blowing of trumpets, throughout the morning. Meantime the whole house was fragrant with the smells of cooking turkey, and sweet potatoes, and boiled onions, and chili sauce, and homemade chow chow, and doughnuts, and pumpkin pie, and plum pudding, and pound cake, and caramel cake, and jumbles (all cut in fancy shapes) and - but there, the list is long enough to make any one's mouth water, and that isn't fair. Needless to say, the children didn't try all of the list, though they would have been quite willing, but Mother made rather a good selection for them. Anyway, the smells and tastes of that fine dinner seemed to go very nicely with the wreaths in the window and the bright red berries. But where was the Tree? It had vanished - probably in the parlor.

They couldn't go in - oh, no - not yet. And after Mother had washed all the thousand and one dishes, helped by Black-eyed Susan - not Black-eyed Susan who lived in the pasture, but the one who lived in the cabin on the canal - she entered the parlor, closing the door very carefully so they couldn't get even a glimpse of what was inside. It was funny how Mother found time to do all the things she did that day - yes, and all the week and month before it. Her hands, Marmaduke said, were like the magic hands in the "Arabian Nights," and he was right. At least the Toyman said, -

"You can bet your bottom dollar on that, my son."

All of which was very strange, when Marmaduke didn't have any pennies even, in his bank, bottom or top, having spent them on surprises for Mother and all the rest of the folks. Nice surprises they were, too. In fact, it was really nicer planning them out, and getting them with the money he had earned, than dreaming about what he would get himself.

The parlor door was kept carefully locked all that long afternoon. The children tried to play with the things that had come in their stockings, but somehow these didn't seem as interesting as what they guessed was going on behind the closed door. So they kept their eyes glued there, as Marmaduke's story-book said, though he thought that was funny, when they hadn't put any mucilage on them.

Once in a while Mother would come out of the parlor to look in the big closet, then she would journey back very quickly, holding the mysterious parcel tight under her apron or shawl so that they couldn't see it. She would open the door, too, only the tiniest crack, to slip in sideways like a slender fairy. And though a radiance and splendor would shine through - like Heaven it was - they could never see what made it, and before they could say "Jack Robinson," the door would be shut -

tight shut - and - that was all.

"Oh, oh," it was so hard to wait!

At last - about four in the afternoon - the signal was given. The Toyman made them all form in line in the dining-room, Mother leading, to show them the way, though they hardly needed a guide; poor little Mrs. Cricket next, for it wouldn't be Christmas unless they made someone outside their own family happy; then Jehosophat, Marmaduke, and Hepzebiah - no, that is wrong, Hepzebiah ahead, as the boys had decided on "ladies first"; then Father and the Toyman, carrying little lame Johnny Cricket on his shoulder; and Black-eyed Susan bringing up the rear - a very big rear she was, Father said, for Susan weighed considerably more than her heaviest clothes-basket.

And so the doors opened!

"Glory be!" sang out Susan, and in that she expressed the feelings of every one in the long procession that entered the parlor. It *was* "glory" - that light, that shining, that radiance! Wreaths in the window, festoons overhead, presents heaped up in the corner and on the floor - and the Tree, the Tree!

It was covered with golden ornaments, and red and silver and blue, and it was draped with strings of popcorn and festoons of red cranberries, flung so gracefully over it, and everywhere, between the green twigs of the spruce and the red, and the gold, and the blue, and the silver of the ornaments and festoons, scores of little candles were shining brightly, twinkling like the stars - like very Heaven come down to earth before their eyes.

Life has many happy moments and many happy times to offer, but nothing more wonderful than a beautiful shining tree bursting on the sight after one has waited all day, no - really for weeks and months.

For ten minutes they all stood and gazed at that tree. Mother and Father were smiling happily; Susan clasped her hands and very properly said "Glory" again; the children danced; Mrs. Cricket wiped the corners of her eyes with her rusty-black shawl; and little Johnny Cricket just sat there in delight.

But where was the Toyman now? He had disappeared as mysteriously as had the tree after they brought it home. He must have forgotten something important, for he couldn't want to do *chores* when there was that tree to look at.

However, the boys were eager enough, both yelling:

"Now for the presents!"

"Wait a minute, laddies," said their father, "somebody's calling."

Now there was a telephone in the White House with the Green Blinds by the Side of the Road, a funny old-fashioned instrument, but a very useful one, nevertheless.

It was tinkling. Father went to it, and this is what they heard him say, -

"Hello! hello!" Then, -

"Why, is that *you* - "

He turned around to the folks in the room:

"Hush!" he warned them, "it's Santa Claus."

Then he turned to the telephone again, very surprised to be talking to so important a person.

"I'm certainly glad to hear from you. How are you?" said Father.

And he whispered to the boys: -

"He says he's very well, " - then into the 'phone: -

"That's fine - we're very glad to hear it."

There was a pause, and Father's voice exclaimed, -

"What! You're not actually coming here? Well, I should say that's the best news I've heard in a long time!"

And, smiling, he told this good news to the folks in the room.

"Doesn't it beat all!" he said, "Santa Claus is coming here to pay us a visit."

He spoke into the 'phone again.

"How soon can you make it? - Fifteen minutes?"

He looked at his watch.

"Of course - we'll wait for you."

Then he hung up the receiver.

"As long as Santy will be here so soon, we'd better wait till he comes, and let him distribute the presents, don't you think?"

He paused a minute, trying to remember.

"Let me see - when was it I last saw him? - yes, yes - it's all of forty years. I was just a little shaver then. I wonder if he's changed much, or grown much older."

As for the children, they could hardly think, much less talk. They sat there, almost in a daze, blinking and looking at the little candles, which seemed to wink back at them as if they had been in the jolly secret all the time.

The youngsters had hardly gotten over their wonder and bewilderment, when they heard sleighbells, and a loud "Whoa - whoa - you old reindeer, whoa when I tell you!" Then there was a stamping on the porch and the old brass knocker was lifted - it fell - "clack, clack"; the door opened, and in walked the welcome guest.

Have you yourself ever seen Santa Claus, or only pictures of him? Well, he really looks like his pictures, only more human - like people you know and love, though of course more magnificent.

In the first place, he wasn't so fat - he was plump in the stomach, but not so really round all over as in the old pictures of him. But perhaps that is because when they were taken there weren't so many children in the world to make things for, and he has grown just a little thinner since then, being so busy, you know.

However, he had on the same red coat trimmed with white fur, the long beard falling down over his chest, and the belt, and the rubber boots, and the red woolen cap on his head. But his face had lost a little flesh, and it wasn't all red as you see in the pictures, but brown and red, - like - like - the Toyman's; and his eyes didn't pop out of his head either, but were just like ordinary people's eyes, only kinder, like the Toyman's, and these, the children said, were the kindest in the world.

Marmaduke wished the Toyman would come back, so that he might meet Santa, for he was a year-round Santa himself, always making things and doing things for little boys.

But Santa was talking:

"Merry Christmas! Merry Christmas!" he said, then he added, - "to one and all."

At the sound of his voice the children forgot their wonder and awe, and hurried to him and clasped his knees, and little Johnny Cricket tried to reach for his crutches, but Santa just picked him up in his arms and kissed him and little Hepzebiah too.

Now Father stood up.

"Mr. Santa Claus," he began, but Santy interrupted him, -

"No Mister for me," he told Father, "we're among friends. I've known you all ever since you were born. Ho! Ho!" and he laughed, and his laugh seemed very jolly.

"Very well," replied Father, "pardon my mistake - Friend Santy, then. Would you be so good as to distribute the presents?"

"Deelighted!" said Santy with a bow, "Marmaduke, you hand 'em to me and I'll read off the names."

So Marmaduke got down on his knees near the pile of presents and picked out one. It was one of his own - not one *for* him but one he had bought - for Mother. He couldn't wait to see that look he knew would come in her eyes.

She opened it. It was a nice work-basket.

"And my little boy bought it all with the pennies he saved. - I know that," she cried in delight, and that look he had waited for shone in her face.

Then came a big long box which Santy handed to Hepzebiah. Santy himself helped her to tear off the wrappings; and lo and behold! it was a great big doll with blue eyes and flaxen hair.

So back and forth the procession of presents passed, - a pipe for Father, and one for the Toyman, who wasn't there to get it, a football for Marmaduke, a pair of skates for Jehosophat, and oh, so many things!

Then Marmaduke heard a whisper in his ear. He started, for the voice sounded like the Toyman's, but it couldn't have been, for the Toyman was still nowhere to be seen.

"Can't you find something in that heap o' things for little Johnny Cricket?" the voice asked.

Marmaduke turned round, to discover Santy whispering in his ear. And he looked hard, and, sure enough, over in the corner was a great big parcel, marked, "Johnny with a merry Christmas." Santy undid it, and revealed a wagon with handles that could be worked by the arms. It looked very much like the Toyman's invention. And it was just the thing for Johnny, who was so lame.

When he saw it he just clasped his hands, and this time the tears did really come, and they ran from the corners of his eyes and down his cheeks. But they were very happy tears.

"You're all so good to me," was all he said.

Marmaduke didn't need Santy to remind him now, and he hunted hard again and found something for "Mrs. Cricket from her friends in the White House," - a fine alpaca dress. There was something for Black-eyed Susan too. And all under that roof and around that tree were very happy. It was too bad the Toyman wasn't there to enjoy it.

Now Santy stood up and looked at his watch. It was a great big one with a ship on its face and an anchor on the chain. It resembled the Toyman's, and the children thought it odd that there were two such watches anywhere in the world.

"It's getting late," Santa was saying, "I've got a lot of places to visit, but before I go, I want you to sing a song - every man Jack."

So together they sang "Peaceful Night, Holy Night," and it sounded very sweet and pretty and made them all think of what Christmas meant, besides just the giving and receiving of presents.

"Now the youngest ones - all together now!" and Jehosophat, Marmaduke, Hepzebiah, and little Johnny Cricket sang, without the grownup people this time:

"Alone in the manger,
No crib for a bed,
The little Lord Jesus
Lay down his soft head."

And that song sounded even prettier and sweeter than the other, with those little voices singing it around the tree and all its candles.

When they had finished, Santa said "Goodbye," and, "Merry Christmas to one and all," bowed, closed the door behind him, stamped his feet, and whistled to his reindeer. Then the sleighbells sounded, growing fainter until they faded quite away.

About ten minutes after he had gone, the Toyman appeared. It certainly was a shame he had to just miss him like that.

Marmaduke called, -

"Oh, Toyman, you missed him - Santy was here."

"He was, was he?" the Toyman replied, "I *am* sorry, for I'd like to have paid my respects to the old fellow."

The funny thing about it was that he didn't seem half as

disappointed as the children - that is, Marmaduke and Hepzebiah, particularly Hepzebiah. Jehosophat just smiled in a sort of superior way and said nothing, but perhaps that was because he was getting older and had lost some of his enthusiasm. As for Marmaduke, he hadn't been so enthusiastic about seeing Santa Claus ever since Reddy Toms had told him something, but now, after seeing Santa alive and before him - why, he didn't care what any "ole Reddy Toms" said.

He had seen Santy - and had shaken him by the hand.

XIV

THE HOLE THAT RAN TO CHINA

By this time you should have noticed, if you ever stop
to think, that Marmaduke was quite a traveller. It was
really remarkable the trips and voyages that boy took -
not only to the town, and Apgar's Woods, and the
Leaning Mill on Wally's Creek, but to the South Seas,
The Cave of the Winds, the Ole Man in the Moon, the
Fields of Golden Stars, and to all sorts of beautiful
cities and kingdoms, some of which you may find in
your geographies, and some not on any map in the
world. And he didn't have much money for fares,
either. It was hard to tell just how he managed all these
journeys, but sometimes, do you know, I suspect he
paid for his fare with a ticket of dreams. What do you
think? Well, anyway, one day he went to China.

And this is the way it all came about:

First he went to town - with the Toyman, of course,
and Old Methusaleh. That old white horse was tied to
the hitching-post in front of Trennery's Grocery Store,
with his nose deep in a feed-bag. While the Toyman
was talking to Mr. Trennery - Mr. Will Trennery, and
his brother Lish - Marmaduke sat on the seat of the
buggy and watched the people. There were a lot of
them, more than he ever saw on the farm, all at one

time. There must have been almost fifty on the street. Some of them were lounging around the soldier who stood on the big stone with a gun that never went off; some were hitching up their horses, or "giddyapping" to them; while a crowd was going in the side door of the "City Hotel," and another stood in front of Trennery's Grocery Store, telling who'd be the next president. They were very wise, they thought, but Marmaduke was sure the Toyman could tell them a thing or two - and that was just what the Toyman was doing.

After a while Marmaduke tired of listening to all their talk about presidents and the new Justice of the Peace, and he looked at the other stores and all their signs. He noticed a new one that had just come to town. It stood between Trennery's and Candlemas' Emporium, and it was even more interesting than the candy store. It had a red sign above the door with white letters which read: -

"Hop Sing
Laundry."

In the windows were parcels of shirts, tied with white string, with little slips of paper under the string. These slips of paper were colored like the petunias in Mother's garden, and on them were funny black letters that looked like chicken-, and rabbit-, and fox-tracks, all mixed up.

Inside the store three little men were ironing, ironing away on boards covered with sheets, and jabbering in a strange language. And they wore clothes that were as strange as the words they spoke - clothes that looked like pajamas with dark blue tops and light blue trousers. And each of the little men had a yellow face, slant eyes, and a black pigtail.

It was Saturday, and a group of town-boys stood around the door, gazing in at the three strange little men and mocking them: -

"Ching, ching Chinaman,
Bow, wow, wow!"

Then one of the boys would shout in through the door, - "Bin eatin' any ole stewed rats, Chinky?" and another would ask, - "Give us a taste of yer bird's-nest pudding?" They thought they were very smart, and that wasn't all, for, after calling the Chinamen all the names they could think of, the boys reached down into the ditch, which some men were digging for a sewer, and scooped up handfuls of mud and threw it straight into the laundry and all over the snow-white shirts the little men were ironing; at which, the Chinamen grew very angry and came to the door, shaking their flat-irons in their hands and calling, -

And the boys ran away, still mocking them. You could hear their shouts dying away in the distance: -

"Chinky, chinky Chinaman,
Bow, wow, wow!"

Not long after this the Toyman came out from Trennery's and climbed on the seat; and he and Marmaduke and Old Methusaleh jogged along towards home. All the way, Marmaduke couldn't help thinking of the three little men in their blue pajamas and their black pigtails; and he asked the Toyman a lot of questions, even more than you will find in his arithmetic, I guess, all about what those letters on the packages of shirts meant, and if the Chinamen braided their pigtails every night and morning just like girls, and if they really did eat "ole rats," and bird's-nest puddings, and all that.

The Toyman could hardly keep up with the questions; and he hadn't answered them all, either, by the time they reached the White House with the Green Blinds by the Side of the Road.

On the afternoon of that same day, Marmaduke was sitting like a hoptoad, watching the Toyman dig post-holes in the brook pasture. The sun shone so soft and warm, and the cedar posts smelled so nice and fragrant, that he began to feel drowsy. He didn't sit like a hoptoad any more, but lay on his elbow, and his head nodded - nodded - nodded.

Rather faintly he heard the Toyman say:

"Well, that's pretty deep. A little more, and I'd reach down into China."

The little boy rubbed his eyes and looked down into the deep brown hole.

"If you dug a little more," he asked, "would you really go down through the earth, all the way to China - where the Chinamen live?"

"Sure," replied the Toyman, who never liked to disappoint little boys.

"Then," said Marmaduke, "please dig a little more - for - I'd like - to see - where - the Chinamen - live - ." His voice sounded very sleepy.

The Toyman dug another shovelful or two, and all the while the little boy's head kept nodding, nodding in the sun - then - as the last shovelful fell on the pile at his side, he looked down in the hole once more and heard voices - strange voices.

Words were coming up out of that hole, and it seemed to Marmaduke that he could see those words as well as hear them. Now that is a very odd thing, but it is actually what happened - he could both see and hear them - and they looked like the funny music on phonograph advertisements - something like this:

And, way down at the bottom of the hole, he saw three black heads with pigtails that curled upward in the hole like smoke coming from a chimney.

He tried to grab hold of them, but he fell, and Wienerwurst after him, right plump among the pigtails, landing on the three Chinamen way down in the hole, and knocking them flat on their backs until their feet with the funny black slippers kicked in the air.

Then they all got up and rubbed their tummies under the blue pajamas.

"Velly wude little Mellican boy," said the first little Chinaman, whose name was Ping Pong.

"Velly bad manners," said the second, who was called Sing Song.

"You beggy our pardon," the third, whose name was Ah See.

Now Marmaduke intended to do that very thing - that is, beg their pardon, for he was very polite for an American boy.

"I'm very sorry - I didn't mean to hurt you," he explained, "I just fell down that hole."

At this he looked up the sides of the hole. It seemed as if he were at the bottom of a great round stove-pipe, or a well with brown sides. Far, far above him was a little circle of light blue, the top of the hole where he had fallen in.

After he had begged their pardon so nicely, the three little yellow men said, all together, -

"Little Mellican boy velly politely; he has honorable ancestors."

Marmaduke looked around again and saw that they were standing, not on the bottom of the hole, but on a little landing like that on a stairway. Below them the hole kept on descending into the darkness, curving round and round like a corkscrew or the stairways in old castles - down, down, down.

"Little Mellican boy like see China?" asked Ping Pong.

"Very much, thank you," replied Marmaduke, trying to be as polite as they were.

But the Toyman would miss him. He looked way up at the circle of light at the top of the hole and shouted:

"Say, Toyman, can I go to China - just for a little while?"

The Toyman's face appeared in the circle of light at the top.

"Sure, sonny, have a good time," he shouted back, and his voice coming way down that hole sounded hollow, as if he were hollering down a well.

Marmaduke waved to him.

"Goodbye, I won't be long," he called.

Then, turning, he saw that the three Chinamen had flat-irons in their hands. They were fitting the handles to them. Ah See handed Marmaduke a fourth iron for himself.

"Mellican boy wide on this - now, velly caleful," said he.

"But how can I ride on such a small iron?" asked Marmaduke.

"Watchee and see,
Allee samee as me."

And at once all the three little Chinamen mounted the irons and curled their tiny slippered feet under them. And Marmaduke curled up on his iron just as they did.

"Allee weady!" shouted Ping Pong, and all-of-a-sudden they started scooting down that curving brown hole, round and round, down through the deep earth. Wienerwurst had no iron to slide on, but he did pretty well on his haunches, and how swiftly the brown sides of the earth slipped by them! How fast the air whistled past!

Robert Gordon Anderson

After a fine ride they saw ahead of them a great red light. It looked like the sky that time when Apgar's barn was on fire.

They stopped with a bump and a bang. Marmaduke waited until he had caught his breath, then he looked around. They had stopped on a gallery, or sort of immense shelf, that extended around a tremendous pit or hole in the earth. In the centre of it stood a big giant, shovelling coal in a furnace. The furnace was as high as the Woolworth Building in New York City, which Marmaduke had seen on picture post-cards. And the Giant was as big as the furnace himself.

He had a beard, and eyes as large and round as the wheels of a wagon; and he was naked to the waist. Great streams of sweat, like brooks in flood-time, poured off his body. When these rivers of sweat struck the ground, they sizzled mightily and turned into fountains of steam that rose in the air like the geysers in Yellowstone Park, it was so hot in the place.

Marmaduke felt pretty warm himself, and he mopped his face with the handkerchief which he had won in the Jack Horner pie at the church sociable. It had pictures of pink and blue ducks and geese on it, and it looked very small beside the handkerchief with which the Giant was mopping his face. That was as big as a circus tent. Marmaduke himself looked very small beside the stranger. When the little boy stretched out his hand, he just reached the nail on the Giant's great toe.

The three little yellow men were exclaiming: -

Which meant that this was the centre of the Earth.

"But what is he doing that for - shovelling all that coal in the furnace when it's so hot already we're most roasting!" complained their little American guest.

His voice was almost lost in the tremendous place. It was strange that it ever reached the Giant's ear, which was hundreds of feet above Marmaduke's head, but nevertheless the Giant did hear it, for he called: -

"Now, you three Chinamen keep your jabbering tongues still," he said, "and let me have a chance to talk. It's so long since I've seen a boy from up on the Earth that I'd like to talk a spell myself - to limber up my old tongue. It's grown pretty stiff all these years."

Then he looked way down at Marmaduke, who was standing there, no higher than the Giant's great toe.

"Come up," he invited the boy, "and have a seat on my shoulder."

Marmaduke looked up and hesitated, for the distance up to that shoulder was so great. He might as well have tried to climb a mountain rising straight up in the air. But the Giant helped him out.

"Don't be scared," he said, "I'll give you a boost."

And he reached down his mighty hand and placed it under the seat of Marmaduke's trousers. The little boy looked no bigger than the kernel of a tiny hazelnut rolling around in the big palm. But very gently the big fingers set him on the tall shoulder, way, way above the bottom of that pit, but very safe and sound. Marmaduke grabbed tight hold of one of the hairs of the Giant's beard to keep from falling off. He had hard work, too, for each hair of that beard was as stout and as thick as the rope of a ship.

"Kind of cosey perch, ain't it?" asked the Giant.

Now it didn't strike Marmaduke as quite that, when he had such hard work to hold on, and he was so far from the ground, but nevertheless he answered, -

"Y-y-yes, s-s-sir."

His lip quivered like the lemon jelly in the spoon, that time he was so sick. If he had fallen from that shoulder, he would have dropped as far as if he had been thrown from the top gilt pinnacle of the Woolworth Building. And so tremendous was the Giant's voice that when he talked the whole earth seemed to shake, and Marmaduke shook with it as if he were blown about by a mighty wind.

"Now," the Giant was saying in that great voice like thunder, "you want to know what I'm heating up this furnace for?"

"Y-y-yes," replied Marmaduke, his lips still trembling like the lemon jelly.

"You see it's this way," the Giant tried to explain, "my old friend, Mr. Sun, keeps the outside of the Earth warm, but I keep the inside nice and comfy."

It seemed strange to hear the Giant use that word, "comfy." It is a word that always seems to sound small, and the Giant was so huge.

"I haven't seen my chum, Mr. Sun, for quite a spell,"

the Giant went on, "let me see - it was the other day when I last saw him."

"What day?" asked Marmaduke, "last Sunday?"

"Oh, no, a little before that. I guess it was about a million years ago."

"A million! Whew!" Marmaduke whistled. "That was quite a long time."

"Oh, no," responded the Giant, "not as long as you think. No more than three shakes of a lamb's tail - when you come to look at it right."

"But where do you get all the coal?" was Marmaduke's next question. "I should think you'd use it all up quick, you put on such big shovelsful."

"See there," the Giant said, for answer pointing in at the sides of the pit. Little tunnels ran from the sides into the dark Earth. And in the tunnels were little gnomes, with stocking caps on their heads, and they were trundling little wheelbarrows back and forth. The wheelbarrows were full of coal, and when they had dumped the coal on the Giant's pile they would hurry back for more. In their foreheads were little lights, and in the dark tunnels of the Earth these shone like fireflies or little lost stars.

"Would you like to see a trick?" asked the Giant.

"A card trick?" asked Marmaduke in turn, rather hoping it was.

The Giant laughed and looked down at his fingers.

Each one was as big as a thick flagpole thirty feet long.

"What would these fingers be doing, playing cards?" he said. "Pshaw! I couldn't play even Old Maid - or Casino."

"I'll show you how," said Marmaduke eagerly, and the Giant put him on a shelf of the Earth close to his head. Then Marmaduke took from his pocket a little pack of cards and shuffled them. He explained the rules very carefully - Old Maid it was - and then dealt them to Ping Pong, Sing Song and Ah See, for they joined in the game, and to the Giant. In those thirty-foot fingers the tiny cards looked like little bits of pink confetti. The Giant seemed to like the game, but Marmaduke beat the three little Chinamen, and the Giant, too, for all he was so big.

They had finished the second hand, when the Giant loo ked at his furnace.

"There, that's what I get for loafin'," he said, "my furnace is 'most out."

After he had thrown about a thousand shovelfuls or so on the fire, which must have taken him all of five minutes, the Giant turned to Marmaduke.

"I haven't shown you *my* trick," he said, "how would you like to see me make a volcano blow up?"

Marmaduke was a little frightened, but it was too good a chance to miss.

"Yes, thank you," he replied, "that would be rather nice."

"Well, sir, watch then."

And the Giant raised his hands to his mouth and shouted at the little gnomes: -

"Hurry, more coal now - make it snappy!"

And the gnomes ran back and forth from the coal-piles to the tunnels, trundling their wheelbarrows, until their legs twinkled under them as fast as the little lights in their foreheads.

Soon the coal-pile was as high as a black mountain, and the Giant began to shovel, shovel away, throwing the coal into the mouth of the furnace which was as high as the Woolworth Tower. Then he closed the door and watched.

The flames began to leap, and the steam began to hiss, and soon the great furnace began to shake all over with the steam imprisoned inside, just like a man with chills and fever. Then all-of-a-sudden, from somewhere above them on the outside of the Earth, they heard a great roar.

"There goes old Vesuvius," said the Giant.

There was another great roar.

"And there's Aetna and Cotopaxi," he added, "now for Old Chimborazo!"

Marmaduke remembered enough of his geography to know that the Giant was calling off the names of the great volcanoes of the world. It was indeed very thrilling! But he really had hardly time to think, for he had to hold on so tight to the rope hair of the Giant's beard; and if the three little Chinamen hadn't kept tight hold, too, of their flatirons, they would have been blown to the ceiling of the pit, the furnace and the whole place shook so. As it was they were tossed head over heels, their feet flying in the air, but their hands held on to the flatirons like ships to their anchors, and they were saved.

The Giant turned to Marmaduke.

"Have you the time?" he asked, "I've broken the watch my grandfather gave me."

Marmaduke took out his little Ingersoll with one hand, meanwhile holding on with the other to the beard.

"It's just twelve," he informed the Giant.

"Noon again - my, how Time does fly!" the Giant exclaimed. "It seems as if yesterday were the *first* noon, and yet that was a couple of million years ago. But we've had only six volcanoes. We must have six more for a noon whistle, so the little gnomes will know it's time for lunch."

There were six more gigantic explosions up on the outside of the earth, then the little gnomes all stopped work, turned up their wheelbarrows, sat down on them in tailor-fashion, took out their lunch-pails, and began to eat. Then the three little Chinamen perched on their irons and took out some bowls and chopsticks. It made the Giant laugh to see their funny antics.

"Ho! ho!" exclaimed he, but he turned away his head in another direction before he laughed.

"I'm laughing in *that* direction," he explained, "because there's a city full of wicked people up there, on the Earth outside. When I laugh, it's an Earthquake, you see, and I don't want to shake up the good people. Now" - he pointed in another direction - "the town of Five Corners is up about there. You wouldn't want me to try an Earthquake on *it*, would you?"

Marmaduke thought this was very kind and considerate of the Giant, to try to spare the people in the town where he went to buy candy and to see circuses and things. Then he had an idea.

"Couldn't you shake up the ground a mile or two west of that - see," he pointed his finger at the roof of the pit, "about there. That's where Fatty lives, over near Wally's Creek, and it would do him good to be shaken up by a earthquake - just a little one."

"All right," replied the Giant, "I can accommodate you. But you're running a risk. I might kill your friend Fatty."

"He isn't any friend of mine," Marmaduke interrupted - then he thought for a moment. After all he didn't really want Fatty killed. He guessed he'd better not take a chance.

"No," he said, shaking his head, "after all, I 'spose you'd better not try it."

"All right," the Giant answered, "just as you say. But have you had any lunch?"

At that question Marmaduke suddenly felt rather faint, and he watched the Giant hungrily, as he took out of an oven in the furnace a dozen steers, roasted whole, and ten loaves of bread, each as big as a house.

It didn't take many gulps for the Giant to swallow the whole lot, but first he very kindly handed a few crumbs of bread to Marmaduke up on his shoulder. At least the Giant thought they were crumbs, but they were really as big as loaves of bread Mother made. And the little slivers of roasted steer which the Giant reached up to him were as big as whole steaks. So Marmaduke's hunger was soon satisfied, and, for once in his life, Wienerwurst's, too.

He wanted to stay a little longer, to talk with the big Giant and ask him questions, but, looking down, he saw the three little Chinamen making odd gestures and beckoning to him with their long fingernails.

"We must hully, quickillilly," they said, which, of course, meant, as you should know, that they had to hurry quickly, or it would be dark before they reached China.

He told his troubles to the Giant, who said he "didn't see what anyone wanted to see that heathen land for," but nevertheless he lifted the little boy down, hundreds of feet to the ground, and Marmaduke curled up on his iron, and the three little yellow men curled up on theirs, while Wienerwurst got down on his haunches; and they all said "goodbye" to the great Giant, and the little gnomes trundling their wheelbarrows, and the little twinkling lights in their foreheads.

On the other side of the furnace, the hole opened up again, and down it they scooted on their way to China. It was fortunate that the Giant had given Marmaduke something to eat, for it was a long trip.

There were many wonderful things there, but as you're all yawning, and we couldn't make sleepyheads understand, for that you'll have to wait till another night.

　　　Robert Gordon Anderson

XV

THE PEPPERMINT PAGODA

After Marmaduke and Wienerwurst, Ping Pong, Sing Song, and Ah See, had scooted down the long hole for a few thousand miles or so, they began to see light below them, a little circle of blue, just at the other end, on the other side of the world. When their long journey was over, they got up from their flatirons and stretched themselves, and Wienerwurst got up from his haunches and stretched himself. Then one by one they stuck their heads out of the bottom of the hole to take a look at China.

A very pretty country it was, yet quite strange. The strangest thing about it all was that now, though they were on the opposite side of the world from the White House with the Green Blinds by the Side of the Road, they weren't standing upside down. They could stand up straight, with their heads - not their feet - in the air, and look at the sun, at the bottom of the hole just as they did at the top, on the farm back home.

When all five had climbed out, they found that they were near a great wall. It was built of very old stones and was as wide as a road on top. Several horses could ride abreast on it.

A company of Chinese soldiers with guns and swords guarded the gate, and the three little Chinamen, Ping Pong, Sing Song, and Ah See, were afraid to enter with the American boy. The soldiers might have let Wienerwurst in because he was yellow like themselves, but Marmaduke was much too white.

Of course, he was disappointed, but his disappointment didn't last long, for Ping Pong just clapped his hands, and all three crouched down as boys do when they are playing leapfrog, or like the acrobats in the circus. Sing Song climbed on the back of Ping Pong, and Ah See on top of Sing Song. But at that Ah See's head reached only half way up the great wall.

He leaned down towards Marmaduke.

"Come up, little Mellican boy," said he.

And Marmaduke climbed up on the three backs and stood on the shoulders of Ah See, who exclaimed in delight to his friends, -

"Why, he not flaidlily at all."

Then he told Marmaduke to catch hold of his pigtail. Which the little boy did, and Ah See swung his head round and round, and his pigtail with it, like David's slingshot in the Bible story.

When the little boy was spinning around through the air, fast as fast as could be, Ping Pong cried, -

"Velly fine - now - one-two-thlee! let him go!"

Marmaduke obeyed instantly, letting go of the pigtail

and flying through the air like a shot. The three little Chinamen all tumbled in a heap at the foot of the wall, but Marmaduke flew over on the other side and landed safely on his feet, inside the great country of China.

He was pleased to see little Wienerwurst, whom the soldiers had let in through the gate, wagging his tail right beside him; and soon the three little Chinamen came running up, too, and one and all started to explore this great country of China.

As far as their eyes could see, stretched green valleys and blue hills under a pale silver sky, and thousands of men and women, as little and as yellow as Ping Pong, Sing Song and Ah See, worked among the tea-fields on every side.

"See that bush," said Ping Pong, "some day Mellican boy's mother drink cup tea from that. Taste velly fine too."

"And this bush," he went on, pointing to another, "make cup for Missee F-f-f-" - he found it hard to say that name - "for Missee Fizzletlee."

And Marmaduke thought it quite wonderful to see the very tea plants which his mother and Mrs. Fizzletree would drink up some day, on the other side of the world, twelve thousand miles away. But there was something else to think about. Trouble seemed to be in the wind. For a little way ahead of them, up the zigzaging white road, they saw an odd-looking group of men. They had swords curved like sickles, hats like great saucers turned upside down, and fierce eyes, and drooping mustaches. Their finger nails were six inches long and stuck out, when they talked, like the claws of wild beasts.

All the people working in the tea-fields hid under the bushes when they saw those men. Only the tea-bushes didn't help them much, for they were so frightened that their little pigtails rose straight up in the air like new shoots growing out of the bushes. There were thousands of those pigtails sticking up straight in the air all over the fields. As for the three little friends, Ping Pong, Sing Song, and Ah See, they trembled like leaves in the wind, then threw themselves flat on their bellies in the dusty road.

"Who are those fellows?" asked Marmaduke, beginning to be frightened.

"It's Choo Choo Choo and his gang, allee velly bad men," explained Ping Pong, though he found it very hard to say anything, his teeth chattered so.

The wild men with hats like saucers turned upside down and the long mustaches and fingernails, came near. Four of them had big poles laid over their shoulders. From the poles hung a funny carriage like a hammock-swing with beautiful green curtains. It was called a "palanquin." When they reached the place where Marmaduke stood, they let the palanquin down on the ground, and he heard a terrible swearing going on behind the green curtains.

The curtains opened, and out stepped a man, also with a hat like a saucer turned upside down, only it was made all of gold and had precious stones in its rim. And his eyes were fiercer, his mustaches longer than those of the other men. In fact, his mustaches reached almost to his knees, and he kept pulling and tugging at them with fingernails that were fully a foot long. My! if those fingernails ever reached Marmaduke's eyes there wouldn't be much of them left. That's what Marmaduke was thinking. And they were very much frightened - all except Wienerwurst, who was smelling the funny slippers of the wild strangers.

Choo Choo Choo (for that was their leader's name) stretched himself. With his drooping sleeves and foot-long fingernails, he looked like the bats that sail under the trees in the twilight and nest, so they say, in people's hair. He gazed out over the tea-fields and saw not a soul, for every mother's son and mother's daughter, too, was hiding tight under the bushes, but a million little pigtails trembled in the air.

"Whee!" shouted the great Choo Choo Choo;

And again, -

"Whee!"

And once more, -

"Whee!"

The million pigtails shook more wildly each time until, at the last, the million little Chinamen rose up from their hiding-places under the bushes, and came running from all over the fields like the inhabitants of a great city running to a fire.

When they reached the road and the green palanquin, they fell on their knees, jabbering and praying the chief Choo Choo Choo not to hurt them with his long curved sword or the curved fingernails, which were worse than the sword.

"Pss-ss-iss-ssst!" exclaimed Choo Choo Choo, who for all his faults liked to see people brave and not cowardly like that.

"Psss-sss-iss-sst!" he said again, then a third time, for in China, especially if you are a robber, you must say things three times if you really mean it, or else people won't believe you at all.

So, again "Pss-ss-iss-sst!" said this bold Choo Choo Choo.

At this third dread cry, each of the million Chinamen took out of his pocket a penny, a Chinese penny. And a Chinese penny is rather big, with a hole in the centre, and funny chicken-track letters stamped on it.

Before Marmaduke could have said "Jack Robinson," there were a million of them lying in the road.

Choo Choo Choo scratched his head with his long fingernail. He didn't know what in the world to do with so many pennies.

After some time he seemed to land on an idea, for he beckoned to one of his soldiers with that nail. And when that nail beckoned, it looked like the long claw of a lobster, waving awkwardly back and forth. It would have been funny indeed, if it hadn't been quite so dangerous.

Nearby a kite flew high in the air, its string tied to a tea-bush. Choo Choo Choo's servant hauled in the kite and the twine, and one by one the soldiers strung all those pennies, those pennies with holes in them, on the twine, like beads on a string.

When they had finished, the string of pennies looked like a great shiny bronze snake coiling back in the road for almost a mile.

By this time the great robber chief Choo Choo Choo had begun to notice Marmaduke.

"Come here!" he commanded, crooking a fingernail. It was funny how Ping Pong, Sing Song, and Ah See, who were quite honest, spoke broken or Pigeon English, while Choo Choo Choo talked correctly and very politely. Robbers, and burglars too, frequently do that. So you can't always tell a man by his fine language.

Marmaduke obeyed. He drew near the palanquin and waited, his heart banging against his ribs.

"What are you doing here?" asked Choo Choo Choo.

"I want to see China."

"Oh you do, do you!" said the robber chief, "and why, pray, do you want to see China?"

"I wanted to see if the people stood upside down on the other side of the world," explained Marmaduke, hoping that this explanation would please Choo Choo Choo.

"So," said he very sarcastically, "that's silly - immeasurably silly, I call it. Look out or you'll go back without a head yourself. But first tell me, - have you any ancestors, *honorable* ancestors?"

"What *are* ancestors, honorable ancestors, sir?" Marmaduke inquired. He thought that if he said "sir" - very politely - it might help matters a bit.

"Oh, people in your family who lived long before you, and who have long beards and are very honest," returned the robber chief.

Marmaduke thought it was odd, his mentioning that honorable ancestors must be honest, when he was a robber himself, but anyway he was relieved as he thought of "Greatgrandpa Boggs."

"Yes," he told Choo Choo Choo, "if that's what it is, I have an honorable ancestor - Greatgrandpa Boggs. He was very old before he died. He was so old his voice sounded like a tiny baby's, and he had a beard - a long and white one - that nearly reached to the bottom button of his vest, and he must have been honest, 'cause Mother said he might have been rich if he hadn't been so honest."

"But wait a minute," roared Choo Choo Choo, "did he have fingernails as long as mine?"

"No," replied Marmaduke, "they were short like these," and he showed him his own hands.

"Pss-ss-iss-sst!" said Choo Choo Choo in disgust, "he couldn't have been so very honorable then. I guess we'd better behead you without any more argument."

He looked around at the sky and so did Marmaduke. It was very pretty and blue, and the road looked very white and inviting, the tea-bushes very lovely and green.

"It's just the right weather for beheading," remarked Choo Choo Choo, "soldiers, are your swords very sharp?" and he patted the snake made of pennies that curved up the white road.

Marmaduke was certainly in danger now, but he kept his head so as not to lose it. And he found an idea in it.

The idea was this: -

Before he had left the Coal-Giant in the Pit in the centre of the earth, the Giant had told him, if he ever needed an earthquake to help him out, to call on him. All Marmaduke was to do was to tap on the earth three times with his right foot, three times with his left, and three times more, standing on his head. Then he was to run away. The Giant had promised to allow five minutes so that Marmaduke and his friends could get to safety.

So this Marmaduke did, just as he had been told. He tapped on the ground three times with his right foot, three times with his left, and three times more, standing on his head, and all under Choo Choo Choo's very nose, for, of course, that was the very place where Marmaduke wanted the earthquake to come.

Choo Choo Choo must have been fooled, for he stopped patting the snake made of pennies, and sharpening his fingernails, and the soldiers ceased whetting their swords. They thought Marmaduke was performing circus tricks for their entertainment.

As soon as he was through standing on his head, he had run away, of course, to get out of the way of the earthquake which he knew would come. But the robbers thought he was just running back to his dressing-room, as all acrobats do, and would come back again for his bow. But he didn't. And after five minutes, just as the Coal Giant had promised, there came a great roar and a mighty tremble, and Choo Choo Choo and all his soldiers were blown up in the air, and when they came down they fell on their heads and knocked their brains out. Then Marmaduke came back - to find them all dead - stone dead.

And he thought it was very kind of the Coal Giant in the Pit in the center of the Earth to help him out with that little favor.

But now all the million tea-Chinamen, who had seen the great happening, fell down on their knees. They thought Marmaduke must have come from Heaven, to work such wonders.

So they dressed him all up in a blue mandarin's coat, which they found in the palanquin. It was covered with pretty snakes, all embroidered in scarlet and gold. And they gave him a cap like a saucer turned upside down and made of gold, and he looked all dressed up for a party.

I guess the million Chinamen thought he did, too, and that they must get up a party for him, for they led him to the great Pagoda which stood on the top of the hill, and which, they told him, was the highest anywhere in the world.

When they reached it, Marmaduke saw that it had

Robert Gordon Anderson

many stories, which grew smaller as they mounted nearer the sky. And each had roofs curving like skis at the end. It was all pink-colored, too, with stripes, and he saw that it was built of peppermint!

He was minded to eat it as Hansel and Gretel had eaten their sugar house, but he didn't, because Ping Pong said it was sacred.

On a throne of stone, inside the Pagoda, sat an old jolly Billiken, also of stone, and shaped just like an egg, with his hands across his tummy and his legs crossed under him.

Now all the million Chinamen had followed Marmaduke, their slippers going "clippity clop," on the pavement of the courtyard. They thought he must be very wonderful to make the earthquake that killed Choo Choo Choo, and they wanted him to sit on the great stone throne of the Billiken. But Marmaduke wouldn't let them. He didn't want to take the seat of the old Billiken when the old fellow had sat there for three thousand years and more.

Billiken, however, had an idea about that. Probably he thought he had been sitting there long enough, for he uncrossed his stone arms from his stone tummy, unwriggled his stone feet, and stood up, stretching and yawning.

"My! but that was a long sleep," he said, and Marmaduke nodded his head. Three thousand years *was* considerable of a sleep.

Then the Billiken stretched out his hand to shake Marmaduke's. The little boy thought it felt very cold, but his new friend's face looked jolly enough.

"Hello!" said the Billiken, "have a game?"

"A game of what Mr. Billiken?" Marmaduke replied.

"Oh, any old thing. What's the latest?"

Marmaduke thought for a moment.

"Well, there's Duck on the Rock," he suggested, "or Roly Poly."

"Duck on the Rock sounds interesting, let's try that."

Then he waved to the other little stone images all around him.

"Come on, fellows, let's play Duck on the Rock. But how do you play it?" he added to Marmaduke, as they reached the courtyard.

"Oh!" replied that little boy, "it's easy. You just place a little rock on a big one, and you each stand on the line with rocks in your hand, an' take turns trying to knock the little one off the big one."

"Suits me," said Billiken, "here, *you*, stand on my head." And he picked up one of the little stone images and set him upon his own head, that was shaped so like an egg.

"Now shoot," he commanded Marmaduke, "let's see how it goes."

And Marmaduke did as he was bid, and he knocked off

the little stone image from the old Billiken's head.

They kept up the game for quite a while, but at last Marmaduke made a wild shot. The rock which he threw went high up in the air and knocked a pink gable off the Peppermint Pagoda.

At this, all the million Chinamen, who had been watching the game respectfully from a distance, set up a howl. They thought it was a sin to smash their pagoda, and that Marmaduke ought to be punished.

So, one and all, they made a rush for him, but again he remembered the Coal Giant's advice. He tapped the ground three times with his right foot, three times with his left, and three times, standing on his head.

Then, after he had run to safety, there came as pretty an earthquake as ever you saw. It didn't kill all the million little Chinamen, but it threw them down on the ground, knocking the wind out of their million tummies completely. And, of course, after that they were very good, being afraid of Marmaduke, as well they might be.

Now, just at this time, the Queen happened by in a magnificent palanquin of cloth of gold. When she saw the trick that Marmaduke had performed, she, too, thought he must have come down from the sky, and she sent her chief officer, the mandarin, to fetch the strange little boy to the Palace.

He was glad to accept the invitation, for he was getting pretty hungry by now. But they had to go through many beautiful grounds with strange summer-houses, and high walls, and ponds with rainbow goldfish swimming in them, before they reached the main part of the palace itself. Then the Queen sat down on her throne, with her mandarins around her, all dressed in those funny coats like pajama-tops and embroidered with red dragons, and gold birds with great wings, and all sorts of queer things.

The Queen seemed a little out of sorts, for, when he came to the throne, she said to him sharply, -

"Show me a trick, or I'll cut your head off."

Marmaduke was puzzled. He didn't know just what to do. He didn't want to start another earthquake. That was only to be used in times of great danger. He'd better try something else first. So he felt in his pockets once more, to see what he could find, and brought out the little pack of cards with which he had played with the Coal Giant.

"I'll teach you how to play" - "Old Maid," he was going to say, but he stopped in time. He thought that maybe the Queen had never been married and she'd be insulted if he asked her to play Old Maid. Then, too, she might insult him back by cutting his head off. And nobody could stand an insult like that. So he just said, -

"*Casino* is a fine game."

But "No," the Queen replied angrily, "I played that long before you were born. And my honorable ancestors played it before me."

Again Marmaduke felt in his pockets, hoping to find something that would help him out. He drew forth a penny, a fishhook, a dried worm, two marbles, and -

there - just the thing - the game of Authors, which Aunt Phrony had given him for his birthday.

"I'll tell you what," he told the Queen, "let's play Authors. There's nothing better than that."

"Authors, authors - " the Queen replied, tapping her foot impatiently, "what are they?"

"Oh, people who write books and stories an' things. It's very nice."

So he explained to the Queen all about them, about Longfellow and Whittier and all the rest. He really didn't know so very much about them, you see, but he had played the game so often that he knew the cards and names "'most by heart."

"Gracious!" exclaimed the Queen - in Chinese, of course. "Whittier and Longfellow - what *pretty* names! But haven't you got Confucius there, somewhere?" Confucius, you see, was a man who wrote in Chinese long years ago, and he was one of her pet authors.

Marmaduke shuffled the cards all over, but couldn't seem to find that name.

"I guess he's been lost," he said politely, so as not to hurt her feelings and lose his head, "but I'll tell you what" - he added, pointing to a picture of Dickens - "we can call this man Confoundit just as well."

"*Confucius, not Confoundit,*" the Queen corrected him crossly, then she looked at the card. "That'll do, I suppose. That author has a kind face and a real long beard. It's not half bad."

She chose Marmaduke for her partner, and they played against the two tallest mandarins in the red dragon coats.

The Queen and Marmaduke beat the old mandarins badly, due to Marmaduke's fine playing. And the Queen was so pleased that she exclaimed, -

"After all, I won't cut off your head. You see, it might stain that pretty rug. I guess we'd better have tea and a party instead." Then she added, - "By the way, do you drink tea?"

"Yes, thank you," he replied, "but make it '*cambric*.'"

"All right if you prefer it," she remarked, "but I call it silly to spoil a good drink that way."

Then she clapped her hands, and her servants came running in, with huge trays of wonderful foods in their arms. And the Queen and the mandarins, Marmaduke and Wienerwurst, and Ping Pong, Sing Song, and Ah See, all sat around the throne, drinking out of the little blue cups and eating the strange food. It made Marmaduke's eyes almost pop out of his head to see the way the Queen and her mandarins, and his three little yellow friends, devoured those dishes, - the stewed rats, the fricasseed shark's fins, and the old birds' nests. Now Wienerwurst didn't seem to object to that sort of food at all, but "licked it right up" like the Chinamen. Marmaduke chose other things instead, - some pickled goldfish, candied humming-birds' tongues, some frozen rose-petals, whipped cloud pudding, and a deep dish of spiced air from the sky, with dried stars for raisins. And, to wash it all down, he had a little blue cup of tea, "cambric" of course, quite as his mother would have wished.

Seeing that he was growing drowsy from such a big meal, the Queen took pity on him and said he could lean back against the golden throne and take a nap.

But first she called the mandarin who was in charge of the Fire-cracker Treasury, where they kept all the finest fire-crackers in the world, and ordered him to bring Marmaduke some. Soon the mandarin came back, and, with him, six servants, with trays heaped high with the prettiest and the fanciest fire-crackers ever boy or man saw. They were wrapped in rose-colored silk paper, with gold letters on the paper, and dragons, too, with great eyes and fiery forked tongues.

The six servants and the mandarin filled all Marmaduke's seven pockets with the packs of fire-crackers, and tied one on Wienerwurst's tail. Then they handed him some bundles of extra-fine punk sticks. It wasn't at all like ordinary punk, but very sweet-smelling.

He lighted one stick, and it smelled so like incense, and he felt so drowsy and nice, that he started to fall asleep. The lighted punk fell lower and lower until it touched one of the fire-cracker-packs. The silk paper began to curl and grow black, then it burst into flames. There was a sputter, then a crackle like the firing of many rifles, and then a great roar. My! but those were powerful fire-crackers. One pack exploded - and he was blown through the palace. Another - and over the Peppermint Pagoda he flew. Still another went off, and he was tossed clean over the Great Wall to the mouth of the hole down which he had come that very same day.

Then the last pack went - *bang*! and he was blown through the hole, Wienerwurst after him, up, up, up, past the Coal Giant and the Furnace Pit, and up, up, up, until he saw, just above him, the little circle of light again.

Out of it he flew - and - all of a sudden his head cleared, and he saw he was sitting back at home once more, sitting against the cedar post, and the Toyman was rubbing his head.

"Never mind," the Toyman was saying, "It'll feel better soon. And how did you like China?"

The head did feel better "pretty soon." Anyway, he didn't mind it a bit. It was worth a headache, as the Toyman said, to have seen the wonderful land of China.

Robert Gordon Anderson

XVI

HE THAT TOOK THE CITY

Marmaduke trudged up the road. And the road went up, up, up the hill. First he thought that road was like a great worm, always squirming ahead of him, but then he decided that, although it twisted, it didn't *squirm*, it was too still for that. After all, it was more like a ribbon, a wide brown ribbon, tied around the green shoulder of the hill.

He wondered where that ribbon road went - over the hill and far away - perhaps clear round the World! But, no, it couldn't do that, for there was the Sea between, and it must stop at the Sea. Anyway, he would have liked to have travelled over it, to the very end, to see all the people and animals that walked over it, and the cities and churches that stood by its side.

But first he must find the Toyman. That is what he had come for. And the Toyman had just gone over that very road. Marmaduke had seen him from the valley below, his long legs climbing up that hill and the little boy had hurried after him, calling and calling.

"'Llo, Toyman, 'llo, Toyman!" he shouted.

He heard an answer and put his hand to his ear to hear

more clearly.

"'Llo, Toyman, 'llo, Toyman!" came the mocking answer, faint and far-away.

But it wasn't the Toyman. It was Echo, calling back from the hills.

Marmaduke had always wanted to meet Echo, but so far he never had. He thought she must be something like the Star-Lady, whom he *had* met, only not quite so bright. Her voice sounded a little sadder, too, like the Bluebird's in the Fall when he says "Goodbye" to the fields and flies to the South. Often he had run after Echo, but he never could catch up with her, nor even see a glimpse of her silver and green dress. She always played Hide-and-Seek with him, and he was always "it."

However, he didn't worry long about friend Echo this morning. He was thinking of the Toyman. For the Toyman's face had looked worried - far away and sad. It had *looked* somehow as Echo's voice always *sounded*. What was it Mother had said? "Poor Frank!" - that's what she called him; "he's in trouble," she had whispered to Father.

Marmaduke didn't know what he could do, but he wanted to catch up with him, and put his hand in his, and tell him not to worry at all, and say, if he needed money he could have all there was in Marmaduke's bank - every last penny, even the bright ones.

Across the road a big jack-rabbit jumped - jumped *sping - sping - sping* - like a toy animal made of steel springs. Wienerwurst ran after the rabbit, but his master didn't stop to chase Jack. He was afraid if he wasted any time he would never catch up with the Toyman.

At last the ribbon road reached the top of the hill and wound along it a little way before it started twisting down the other side. For a moment Marmaduke's eyes followed it down hill, and he wanted to follow it with his legs too, there were so many wonderful and mysterious places where it went, but just then he caught sight of the Toyman.

He was sitting right on the top of the hill, sitting with his chin in his hands, and his eyes on the West far away. And he said never a word.

So Marmaduke just stole up softly, and put his face against the Toyman's, and sat down beside him.

And then the Toyman's eyes came back from far away and looked down on the little boy and smiled again.

"Don't you worry, Toyman," the little boy said to him, "don't you worry about *anything*. It'll all come out in the wash."

The Toyman didn't ask what he meant by that, for he knew it was a proverb, a boy's proverb that was as good as any King Soloman ever made.

"Sure, sonny," he repeated, "it'll all come out in the wash." And he patted the hand beside him.

You see, Marmaduke never asked the Toyman what his trouble really was, or anything at all. And that is always the very best way - when a friend's in trouble, don't bother him with a lot of questions - and pester the life out of him - but just take his mind off his troubles by suggesting some nice game to play - like marbles or "Duck-on-the-Rock," or going fishing, or something; and if you can't do that, just sit beside him, "quiet-like," and be his friend.

For a while they sat so, drinking in the cool air, and looking down at the valley, and the white houses, and red barns, and the yellow haystacks, and the horses and people like ants crawling here and there. There were two ribbons in the valley now, one brown and one silver, the Road and the River. And from the Church with the Long White Finger Pointing at the Sky, came the sound of bells - pealing - pealing - up the hill to the Sky.

All else was still. But after they had listened for a while they discovered that it wasn't so still as it had seemed. Every bird and insect, each leaf and blossom, was busy, preparing its dinner, or else just growing. A twig rustled as a little garter snake squirmed into the thicket. A little gray nuthatch looked for its lunch on a locust tree, crawling over the trunk head-downwards, while, on a branch overhead, a crested flycatcher perched watching, watching, then all-of-a-sudden swooped down and pounced on a fly, swallowed him, flew back to its perch, and watched again.

In the tall grasses which rose like a miniature forest around his head, green katydids jumped, as spry as monkeys. And, as he lay on his back, he could see, way up in the middle of the sky, and right on a line with his eye, Ole Robber Hawk himself, or else one of his relatives or friends. He was brown, of course, but against the blue of the sky he looked like a little black speck with a couple of thin wavy lines for wings.

There was music, too, for a woodthrush sang, oh ever so sweet, and the oriole whistled as clear as a flute, while a locust rattled away like the man who plays the drum and all the noisy things in the theatre-orchestra. But, busiest of all, at his feet an army of black ants hurried around a little hole in the ground, seeming quite as big as the people and horses in the valley below.

"It's just like a little city here, isn't it, Toyman?" Marmaduke said, "all the katydids, and bugs, and snakes, and things, workin' an' workin' away."

"Yes," said the Toyman, as they watched Robber Hawk swing round and round in the sky, "how any one can feel lonely in the country I can't see. I can understand it in the city, where you can't speak to a soul without his putting his hand on his watch, but here there's always a lot of folks with beaks and claws and tails, and all kinds o' tongues an' dialecks, that you don't need any introduction to, to say 'howdy!'"

But Marmaduke remembered that morning and how the Toyman had seemed in trouble. He had certainly looked lonely when Marmaduke and Wienerwurst had found him sitting up there on the hill, and the little boy couldn't help asking, - "Don't you ever feel lonely? You haven't any wife, and Mother says she pities a man without chicken or child - 'tleast she said something like that - and how it wasn't good for a man to live alone - an' *you* do - out in your bunkhouse."

For the first time that afternoon the Toyman, who had been so worried, laughed his old hearty laugh, and

Echo sent it back from her cave in the hill.

"No!" said he, "I don't want any ole wife. Like as not she'd talk me to death. Besides I don't feel lonely when you're along, little fellow."

The little boy felt very happy over that, but, for some reason or other, he felt quite embarrassed, too. Often, when he felt happiest, he couldn't put his happiness into words - he just couldn't talk about the particular thing that was making him happy. And, strange to say, he would usually talk about something quite different. So he said, -

"Let's see your knife."

The Toyman took it out. It was a beauty, too, with *five* blades, all of different sizes, and a corkscrew.

Marmaduke tried to open one of the blades, but he couldn't, they were too strong for his fingers.

So the Toyman took it.

"Which shall it be?" he asked.

"The very biggest," came the answer, "and oh, Toyman, let's play 'Mumbledy Peg!'"

"A galoochious idea!" exclaimed the Toyman, "how did you ever think of it?"

"Oh!" said Marmaduke, "I thought of it - *just like this*"; and he snapped his fingers to show just how quick. "But pshaw! I could think of lots more galoochious than that." Then he added in delight, - "The one who loses has to pull the peg out of the ground with his teeth."

Meanwhile the Toyman was driving that peg into the ground. When it was in so far that it seemed as if no Thirty White Horses could ever pull it out, they began the game - the famous game of Mumbledy Peg.

First, Marmaduke put the knife in the palm of his right hand and made that knife turn a somersault in the air. And it landed right on the blade point and stuck upright in the ground.

Then, taking the knife in the palm of his left hand, he made it turn another somersault in the air. Again it landed on the point of the blade and stuck in the ground, quivering deliciously.

"Neat work!" said the Toyman. Probably he said it too soon, for on the very next try Marmaduke missed, and the Toyman had his turn.

He took the knife and got just as far as Marmaduke with his tricks, then he missed, too.

So Marmaduke took another turn and clenched his right fist tight shut, and threw the knife in the air from that, and it turned another somersault clean, and landed straight up in the ground. And he did the same with his left hand clenched. He was getting on famously!

The next trick in the game of Mumbledy Peg was to twirl the knife from the tip of the first finger, then from the second, and so on. When Marmaduke tried it from the third finger, the knife fell on its point, quivered feebly as if it were sick, then fell over on its side, only part way up in the air.

"Can you get two fingers under it - between the blade and the ground?" said the Toyman eagerly. "If you can, it's all right."

"*You* try?" said Marmaduke.

"What - with *these* fingers?" laughed the Toyman, "you'd better try yours - you'd have more of a chance."

So Marmaduke tried, and just managed to squeeze his two smallest between the blade and the ground. But when he tried twirling it from his last finger he failed. The knife fell over on its side, and he couldn't squeeze any two of his fingers, even the smallest, between the grass and the blade.

"Oh dear!" he exclaimed, "I always miss with my 'pinky.'"

However, the Toyman missed with his fourth finger, and Marmaduke was still ahead.

"I'm off my game," the Toyman explained a little later, as he threw the knife over his left shoulder and failed, "and you're in rare form!"

Now this was strange, for the Toyman was so good at work and games and everything, but I'm thinking it was like that time they played marbles - he did it on purpose, just to let the little boy have the fun of winning. That would have been like the Toyman.

Anyway, the last time Marmaduke threw the knife through the air, and it made its last somersault and stuck up in the ground, straight as straight as could be and quivering like a jews-harp, the Toyman said, -

"Congratulations, ole man, you've won!"

And somehow Marmaduke liked to be called "ole man," and felt quite as proud over that as over winning the game.

Now the Toyman had to get down on his hands and knees and try to pull the peg out of the ground with his teeth. And oh, what a time he made of it, growling like a dog over a bone, all for the fun of the thing, until Marmaduke shouted in glee and Echo answered back from her cave again.

So for a long time they played Mumbledy Peg on the hill, while the shadows grew longer and longer on the grass at their feet. Then they stopped to rest and sat quiet "for a spell."

Opposite them, in the West, were other hills, higher ones too, rising way up in the sky. And far above them curled great white clouds, standing still as still could be.

For a long while they watched those clouds, the man and the boy, then Marmaduke said, -

"I wonder if you see what *I* see."

"What *do* you see, Sonny?" the Toyman replied.

"A great big city - look, there it is!" And the little boy pointed straight at the clouds.

"Why, to be sure!" exclaimed the Toyman, "there it is, an' it looks mighty pretty. But just *what* do you make out?"

"Well!" replied Marmaduke, squinting his eye thoughtfully, "*I* see a big wall and towers on it - a whole lot of towers. There's about fifty, I guess."

The Toyman squinted too, and pointed his brown finger at the clouds, counting slowly under his breath.

"Fifty-*one* towers I make," he said as he finished - "some little and some big; and some have little peaks on 'em, and some are all scalloped out on top."

"And there's a church - a *whopper* of a big one!" went on Marmaduke.

"Where?" asked the Toyman, craning his neck.

Marmaduke pointed at the Cloud City.

"There - just behind the biggest tower."

"Just a little to the right, you mean?" again asked the Toyman, trying hard to see so as not to miss anything in that wonderful city. Then he added, - "oh, I get it now - it's got a gold cross on it an' little diamonds at the tips. My! how they shine in the sun."

Then Marmaduke put in, -

"An' there's flags on the towers, red, yellow and blue - "

"How nice they look!" the Toyman murmured, "all a

wavin' in the wind."

"And there's soldiers in the streets, with helmets on their heads, an' spears, an' things -"

"You bet - an' you kin hear the silver shoes of their horses on the cobbles -"

"What kind of cobbles?"

The Toyman thought a moment -

"Oh, let me see - wh-h-y, I'd say they were all cut outo' agate like your shooters - leastways they look like that at this distance. An' the sidewalks, of course, are of gold - a blind man could tell that -"

"What else?" demanded Marmaduke, a little out of breath, and dazzled by all this sudden glory.

"Oh, a lot else - " the Toyman replied, "for one thing, the door-knobs in all the castles are silver - but then that's nothin' - silver's so common even their frying-pans are made outo' that. But you ought to see their lamp-posts in the street. Their poles are built of ivory from the tusks of elephants of the first water; an' the glass on top is nothing but rubies -"

"Whew!" exclaimed Marmaduke, "that's a great city."

"Yes," added the Toyman, "it's a great city."

So for a little while they watched that great Cloud City with all its towers, and flags and banners waving in the wind; and heard the horses prance over the bright cobbles, and the glorious music coming from out the great church doors. Suddenly Marmaduke asked, -

"Do you 'spose we could take that city?"

"'*Spose!*" exclaimed the Toyman, "why, I'm *sure* of it. Just call up your horses an' call up your men." And he put his hands to his lips and hallooed through them as through a trumpet, Echo answering back as if she had a trumpet, too.

"Hurry," the Toyman went on in excitement, "there's your horse - come, put your foot in the stirrup an' lick him up an' away we'll go!"

And he made all the motions of mounting a horse himself, and calling, "Charge!" to the soldiers. It was a beautiful game, and so real that Marmaduke felt he was actually flying through the air on a winged horse, at the head of a mighty column of soldiers, straight towards the Cloud City.

But alas! they didn't take that city, for, as they came near it, a horn sounded from the valley below. They turned back to look and there far, far beneath them, they saw the White House with the Green Blinds By the Side of the Road, and Mother standing by the door. She looked ever so tiny, and she was blowing that horn over and over to call them to supper. They reined in their horses to listen, for they knew what they would hear in a minute. Yes, there it came, that other horn - it was Echo's. And when they turned in their saddles to look at the Cloud City again, it had vanished - vanished at the sound of the horn, with all their horses and men.

"Oh dear!" said Marmaduke, when he found himself

Robert Gordon Anderson

on the hill once more, the game all over and ended, "she's always mocking us an' spoiling things, that Echo. If I ever catch her, I - I'll break her horn an' throw it down the waterfall, so she can't blow it again - *ever*."

"Never mind, sonny, we'll take that city some time," said the Toyman.

"We had a lesson 'bout that, in Sunday school today," Marmaduke told him, "all about 'he who taketh the city.' But the teacher said 'he who conquers his spirit is greater'n he who taketh the city.' How can you conquer a spirit, Toyman, when you can't see it? Did you ever conquer your spirit?"

The Toyman looked very sober for a while, as they rose and turned their faces towards the road and the valley.

"Yes," he said, "that's what I've been trying to do all day. I had some trouble an' temptation, an' it was getting the best of me. You know, something bad in me that was tellin' me to do things I'd oughtn't to. I tried hard to get my fingers around that bad spirit an' throw him out by his heels. That's why I came up here on the hill to fight it out. You'll understand some day - when you're older."

But, strange to say, the little boy thought he understood even then - at least part of it.

"Have you conquered it, Toyman?" he asked at last.

"I think so," the Toyman answered slowly - "leastways I hope so."

"And *when* did you conquer it?" the little boy prattled on.

The Toyman thought for a moment.

"When you just crep' up behind me, so still an' quiet, an' put your face against mine." And at that the Toyman hugged him again. "No, I guess we won't take that city tonight - we've done a better job."

As they walked to the brown ribbon road again, and over the hill to the valley, the sun was setting. They could see it perched like a gold saucer on the top of the hill, or like the shield of one of their soldiers. Gold bit by gold bit it sank below. Then it went altogether, out of sight, but the Cloud City came back again just for a moment, and a rosy light shone upon that Cloud City and all its banners, and towers, and spires.

Then suddenly it faded quite away. And the little boy and the Toyman walked home through the night, but they whistled together as they went.

Robert Gordon Anderson

www.ingramcontent.com/pod-product-compliance
Lightning Source LLC
Chambersburg PA
CBHW030307180626
46810CB00003B/949